W9-BRL-759

CAN'T HEAR YOU LISTENING

ALSO BY HADLEY IRWIN

ABBY, MY LOVE

BRING TO A BOIL AND SEPARATE

I BE SOMEBODY

KIM/KIMI

MOON AND ME

SO LONG AT THE FAIR

WHAT ABOUT GRANDMA?

(Margaret K. McElderry Books)

THE LILITH SUMMER

WE ARE MESQUAKIE, WE ARE ONE

WRITING YOUNG ADULT NOVELS

(WITH JEANNETTE EYERLY)

CAN'T HEAR YOU LISTENING

HADLEY IRWIN

MARGARET K. MCELDERRY BOOKS
NEW YORK

Collier Macmillan Canada
TORONTO

Maxwell Macmillan International Publishing Group
NEW YORK • OXFORD • SINGAPORE • SYDNEY

Margaret K. McElderry Books
Macmillan Publishing Company
866 Third Avenue
New York, NY 10022

Collier Macmillan Canada, Inc.
1200 Eglinton Avenue East
Suite 200
Don Mills, Ontario M3C 3N1

First Edition
Designed by Barbara A. Fitzsimmons
Printed in the United States of America
10 9 8 7 6 5 4 3 2 1

Library of Congress Cataloging-in-Publication Data
Irwin, Hadley.
Can't Hear You Listening / Hadley Irwin.
p. cm.
Summary: Chronicles the changing relationship between Tracy and her overprotective, famous-author mother and Tracy's struggle to help a close friend who's experimenting with drugs.
ISBN 0-689-50513-2
[1. Mothers and daughters—Fiction. 2. Friendship—Fiction. 3. Drug abuse—Fiction.] I. Title.
PZ7.I712Ca 1990 [Fic]—dc20 90-32675 CIP AC

To Jeffrey Alan Magruder

IN MEMORIAM

1

"HURRY UP AND COME LOOK! YOUR MOM'S ON now, and she's wearing your new Guess jacket!"

I wandered back to the den, where Amy was slumped on the sofa staring at the TV. I could hardly bear to look, but I had to. My mother filled the screen, and not only was she wearing my new jacket, she had on my favorite pair of stone-washed jeans. At least the Reeboks were hers. Mine were too big.

"Doesn't she look great?" Amy asked without taking her eyes from the set.

I didn't answer. She didn't look great to me. She looked phony, like a mother trying to pretend she wasn't one.

"How terribly exciting," the interviewer intoned. "How did you feel when you learned your Help Yourself book made the best-seller list? Fantastic, I imagine."

The man was answering his own question. Mom smiled at him, a crooked smile that always signaled danger. "Just as you so aptly phrased it," she said too sweetly. "Fantastic."

"And this is . . . What? Your first book?"

Mom curled one leg around the other and leaned toward the young man. "Shame on you." She reached over and tapped his arm. "You haven't done your homework, have you?"

I closed my eyes. Didn't Mom know she looked as if she were coming on to the guy?

"My first book was *Help Yourself with Anger,* and my second," she explained in that ultrapatient tone she so often assumed with me, "was *Help Yourself with Beauty.* You see, I'm going down the alphabet. This latest is *Help Yourself with Companionship.*"

"Oh, I see." The man snickered. "And I suppose your next will be *Help Yourself* . . . with what? Drama? Danger? Disaster?"

"All of the above." Mom sounded coy now. "It's to be *Help Yourself with Daughters.*"

I opened my eyes.

"Then you have daughters, I assume."

"One. Two would be redundant."

The man looked as if he'd lost his script. "Well, let's take a brief commercial break and we'll come back and explore daughters—or should I say the daughter? We're talking with Welda Spencer, author of the popular Help Yourself series."

Welda Spencer! That wasn't Mom's real name. Her name was Dorothy. She made up Welda from a numerology chart. "I need a name with five letters and it has to start with *W.*"

A dog-food commercial filled the screen.

"How about that, Trace? You're going to be explored! Right on TV." Amy leaned forward, lips pursed like the interviewer's. "Speak into this mike, Ms. Spencer. How does it feel to be explored? Fantastic, I imagine."

That's when I placed Amy on my personal endangered-species list, even though she was my best friend. "It feels," I said, "like *Help Yourself* to a little rum and Coke. Mom's rum. My Coke."

Amy sat up straighter. "Party time without Mary Agnes? She'll kill us when she finds out!"

"So would the famous Welda Spencer, *if* she found out," I said over my shoulder as I headed toward the kitchen.

At sixteen, Mary Agnes, Amy, and I would have been grounded for life by all of our parents if they had ever known that we brightened up some incredibly dull evenings with their unknowing help. Fortunately, they never seemed to check their liquor supplies, and we didn't do it very often, so it really wasn't any big deal.

When I got back to the den with the rum and Cokes, the dog food had turned into deodorant, and if I'd been alone, I would have switched off the TV before the interview started again. Watching Mom gave me that weird feeling that maybe that was the way I'd look and act when I got older. I was ashamed of her, but even more ashamed of myself for being ashamed of her.

"You know, don't you, that Mr. Jackson's taping this for speech class." Amy ran her forefinger around the edge of her pop can. "You're so lucky, Tracy."

"Why? For having a mother?" I didn't need to be reminded that I'd have to sit through speech class next week and watch the whole thing over again.

"For having a mother like her. She's cool." Amy took another tiny sip. She always did that—drank in aggravatingly tiny sips so that she'd still have over half left ten minutes after I'd drunk all of mine. When we were little kids, she did the same thing: licking ice cream down into the bottom of her cone to make it last longer so I'd have to sit and watch her finish.

"I wish she were my mother."

I took two big swallows of my drink. "I'll trade you."

I wasn't serious, really. Partly serious, maybe. I loved my mother, but something happened when I started high school. She changed. I still loved her, but she became harder to like. I think it all began when she got off on this help-yourself kick and joined a consciousness-raising group. Amy's mom with five kids, all girls, preferred to remain unconscious, or at least that's what Amy said.

"You were remarking before the break . . . ," Mr. Question Mark on TV began again, "that your next book will concern daughters, and you mentioned, Ms. Spencer, that you have a daughter."

I wanted to hide. I knew what was coming.

"Yes, I have a daughter, Tracy."

"Tracy? You mean . . . Tracy? Tracy Spencer?" The man's jaw slackened, and he looked at Mom.

"Yes. I married a man named Spencer and it seemed the only logical thing to name a daughter Tracy Spencer." Mom laughed. It was a big joke with her and always had been. Friends like Mary Agnes, Amy, or Stanley, who watched old movies, kidded me now and then about my dumb name, but now everyone who watched TV would be laughing, too. Couldn't Mom understand how that would make me feel? She must have been a teenager herself once, although it was hard to imagine.

"You named your daughter Tracy Spencer sort of as a joke, then?"

"Not really. She looked like a Tracy Spencer." Mom was kidding, but the poor TV host didn't realize it. She often kidded when I wanted to be serious.

"So in this next book that you're thinking of writing, what advice can you give mothers with daughters? If you were to give them one piece of advice, what would it be?"

"Have sons," Mom quipped, then hurriedly added, "No. To be serious, from the research I've done so far and from my own experience, I would have to say all a mother can do is pour in the love and let it come out as it will."

She was making me sound like a sieve.

"And that's the way you raised your daughter . . . your Tracy?"

"We didn't really raise her. We just loved her."

I looked out the window and tried not to listen to the voices. It had been that way once. Our sixth grade even voted her Mother of the Month. That was when she provided Kool-Aid and cookies for Book Week. But in seventh grade it was all downhill. From eighth grade on I never won an argument.

"Why can't I stay overnight with Mary Agnes?"

"Because her parents aren't going to be home. You see, Tracy, I worry about you."

"I bet Grandma Ida let you do things when you were my age."

"That's why I worry, dear."

"Enough about daughters. What about this book *Help Yourself with Companionship?*"

I drained the last of my drink. At least they were off daughters.

"Humans are gregarious by nature, but there must be

space in their togetherness. Like houseplants, relationships, after they have existed for any length of time, need room—need repotting."

Mom was using a false analogy. I learned that in Mr. Jackson's speech class. Relationships and houseplants were alike in only one way and that was not enough to base an argument on. Wait until Mr. Jackson heard that on the tape!

"For healthy growth, your azaleas, geraniums, impatiens must be thinned, pruned, cut back, roots shaken out and placed in fresh, new environs in order to realize full potential."

Furthermore, Mom didn't know anything about plants. No matter how carefully she thought she followed directions, her Christmas poinsettia, her Mother's Day azalea, her birthday African violet yellowed and shriveled after a few days either from lack of water or too frequent waterings, lack of sunlight or too much sun or as Mom said, "They don't cooperate with me."

"So what you are saying is," the TV host repeated, "that periodically one must revitalize a relationship by what you call repotting."

Repotting! Dad called it trial separation. Amy called it parental mid-life crisis.

I called it inconvenient.

The past year, Mom and I had lived in our house on one side of town while Dad occupied the apartment Mom had found for him on the other side. For a while it was really a mix-up with bills and taxes and rent and bank accounts, but all that got straightened out and now they seemed to be in some kind of holding pattern. Only sometimes I felt as if I were the only thing holding them together. I finally decided they were just going through some sort of phase that they'd grow out of sooner or later. Besides, lately I'd discovered there were some perks to the arrangement. Whenever either of them started getting on my case, I could always switch houses for a couple of days.

Amy was laughing at something Mom must have said. I didn't bother to ask what I'd missed. I'd heard sixteen years' worth of Mom's one-liners.

The program finally ended, and Amy clicked off the TV. She hadn't moved since the interview began, but that wasn't unusual. When Amy did move, it was in slow motion. Sometimes when Amy was with me, I forgot she was even around. That can be very comfortable in a friend. To tell the truth, Amy wasn't only laid-back, she was usually completely prone. Mary Agnes claimed Amy had gone beyond being a couch potato. She was a total tuber.

"I have to move it, Trace," only Amy didn't. She settled back into the couch. "I promised Mother I'd be home in time to put the two monsters in their cages. I don't care what you do in your entire life, Trace, but never, never have twins. Or if you do, make sure they're at least eighteen and on their way to college when they're born."

"There are enough mothers in the world already." I was still staring at the empty TV screen. "I intend to remain cerebrate."

I knew *cerebrate* was the wrong word, but it was a game we played for fun. It drove Mom crazy because she didn't know if we were serious or not.

"You mean *celibate. Cerebrate* means to think, so you couldn't remain cerebrate even if you could do it in the first place, which you can't."

"Not thinking is a virus." I threw a pillow at her. "I caught it from you."

Mom was always getting on me for the way Amy and Mary Agnes and I talked to each other. It was another one of our games: to see who could insult the other in the cleverest way. "You don't talk to your friends that way." It was one of Mom's many "don't's."

"At least I don't insult them behind their backs," I muttered so softly she couldn't hear, and I knew it drove Mom crazy.

"What did you say?"

"Oh, nothing." I don't know why, but it was necessary for me to have the last word even though Mom couldn't hear it.

Amy tossed the pillow back. "So what are you doing this weekend? Want to go on a mall-crawl with Mary Agnes and me?" Obviously she was ignoring the prospective bedtime battle with her twin sisters.

"Sunday afternoon, maybe, if I get back in time. Tomorrow is reestablish-family-ties-with-Dad day. I owe him a day in the great outdoors."

Amy crinkled her nose. "Wandering through woods or parading through prairies?"

"I have an awful feeling it's going to be prairies." I didn't bother to ask if Amy wanted to come with us. She could walk for hours through shopping malls, but doing the same thing in fresh air suddenly became exercise, a word that was not included in her vocabulary.

I really sort of liked my weekends with Dad. Dad was not an arguer. Instead he talked—talked about switchgrass that once covered the prairies of the Middle West, why prairie fires were necessary, and why the dream of every wildlife biologist was to find and preserve the tiny tracts of original prairie still in existence.

Amy finally sat up again. "I got to go." She moved toward the door. "Tell your mom she was . . ." She shook her head. "Totally awesome. Are you sure you're not adopted?"

I couldn't think of a return insult right off because there were times when I wished I *were* adopted.

I picked up our empty Coke cans, took them out to the kitchen and rinsed them carefully. I didn't feel like waiting up for Mom. I know it was mean, but I didn't want to talk about her TV program. Maybe it was because she'd worn my clothes or because she'd gotten a laugh about my name or maybe I was just a little bit jealous at the way the interviewer had practically fallen all over her. Anyhow, I locked the doors, turned on the porch light and headed upstairs.

The phone rang just as I reached my bedroom. I figured it was Amy with a good-night insult she'd been saving. Instead, it was Mom.

"Darling."

I opened my mouth to answer, but Mom didn't give me a chance.

"Did you catch the program? I'm going to be late. The crew wants to take me out for something to eat, and there's a man here from the newspaper who wants to interview me. So listen, dear. Don't wait up. Just leave the porch light on and I'll see you in the morning. Bye now."

Mom hung up and left me standing there holding a dead phone. It was just one more example of the way she was changing, as if the whole world revolved around her and she didn't even think of me at all.

Normally on Saturdays I slept until the smell of breakfast pulled me out of bed and sent me down the stairs toward bacon or popovers or whatever Mom was fixing, but this morning Dad was stopping by for me real early, so I'd set my alarm thinking Mom would be the one to sleep in.

I should have known I couldn't outguess a Super Mom. "Hi there. I heard your alarm." Mom was doing Mom like a B movie actress. "What can I fix you for breakfast?"

She could look beautiful even in the morning; in fact, I think she got prettier the older she grew and the older I got, the dorpier I became. I was already two inches taller than she and five pounds heavier.

"You didn't have to get up. I can get my own breakfast."

"I know exactly what kind of food you would have fixed. You'll be back in time for dinner Sunday, won't you?"

She hadn't even combed her hair, but it still looked just as lovely as if she'd been brushing it for hours. I always looked as if I'd been caught in a whirlwind when I crawled out of bed.

"I'll be back. Can we eat out?"

Mom poured herself a cup of coffee, sat down, and propped her feet up in what used to be Dad's chair. "Out? Out on the deck? Out of the house? Or out of a can?"

I refused to answer. People should never try to be funny at six-thirty in the morning, especially mothers.

"Did you watch the interview last night?"

I should have mentioned the TV interview right away

and told her what Amy had said, but I hadn't and I didn't know why.

"Most of it." I gulped down the glass of orange juice she'd poured for me.

"Not all of it?" Mom could do something with her eyes, sort of half close them then open them again, that made you feel two inches tall.

"Amy was here. I had to get a couple of Cokes from the fridge, so I missed a little of it."

"Oh." The toaster popped up with a piece of toast. Mom buttered it, cut the slice into four neat triangles, arranged them on a plate, and brought them over to the table.

"Can I have some jelly?" I could have gotten up and found some in the refrigerator, but Mom was closer. I knew I was acting like a spoiled brat.

"The magic word?"

I couldn't help but grin. "Please?"

"So what did you think?" She set the jelly jar in front of me and sat down across the table from me.

"About what?" I really wasn't listening to her. I was thinking how maybe I could coax Dad into letting me go to the R-rated movie at the mall with Amy.

"About the possibility of North Dakota's seceding from the union." Mom's voice was flat.

"Oh," I answered. "You mean about the interview last night?"

Mom nodded.

"My clothes looked nice. And I suppose you sold a lot of books." I looked at my watch. "Wonder where Dad is? He's late. He said he'd be here at seven sharp."

Mom stood up. "Oh, I forgot to tell you. I'm dropping

you off at his apartment. Are you ready?"

"When did he call? I didn't hear the phone."

Mom grinned down at me. "He didn't. He turned up last night at the TV station. He knew I'd be nervous."

I couldn't believe it! She was actually blushing!

2

HAVING A PART-TIME, REPOTTED FATHER wasn't bad. I didn't see him much less than I had before, but now he talked to me as if I was a human being instead of just an addition to his and Mom's lives. Not only did he talk, he even listened, at least most of the time. Unlike Mom, he wasn't always peering over my shoulder and asking uncomfortable questions.

Dad was in the shower when I got to his apartment, so I sat down on his futon to wait. The place looked like a motel room, as if no one ever lived there for more than a night or two. The only thing that looked like Dad was the stack of magazines and professional journals beside the one easy chair. Dad was a neatnik: everything in its place, lined up evenly as if standing for inspection. Mom always kidded him that he didn't need a dresser for his socks and underclothes; he needed a file cabinet. Mom didn't need to talk. She was just as bad.

"Hi, Cricket." Dad smelled fresh and soapy as he tousled my hair on the way past. Dad always made me feel important. Maybe all a daughter needed was a father.

"Mom said you saw her program last night. That you went to the studio." I didn't much like the way my voice sounded, but it was too late to do anything about it.

Dad either didn't notice or he ignored what he'd heard because all he said was, "She looked great, didn't she?" and disappeared into the kitchen.

I waited for him and stared at the end table where pictures of Mom and me stared back. Mom looked beautiful; I looked bug-eyed, as if someone had jumped out and scared me just as the camera was snapped. I thought about telling Dad it was dumb to have our pictures when a simple move back across town would give him the real thing. Like awards in a trophy case, all three of Mom's books were lined up beside the photograph.

"Where are we going?" I didn't want to talk about Mom's TV appearance.

"McCray's Prairie. About forty miles north of here. Bob Prentice heard of an area he thought I'd be interested in."

"You mean Stanley's coming, too?"

Dad emerged from the kitchen carrying a Thermos and two paper sacks. Dad's sack-lunches never varied: cold meat sandwiches, apple, two prefabricated cookies and a thermos of milk.

"Of course Stanley's going. He records our data."

Stanley had been around all my life. My baby book was full of pictures of Stanley and me together in our strollers, together in a kids' wading pool, racing together on our new tricycles, coasting down hills on our new sleds, sitting next to each other in kindergarten.

Age had not been kind to Stanley. By fifth grade, I was laid-back. He was uptight. While Amy and Mary Agnes and I organized the Fifth Grade Wreckers, Stanley got A's in Classroom Behavior. Amy maintained he had been born with a clipboard and ballpoint pen permanently attached because he was either recording everything he saw or heard, making lists of things he had yet to learn or keeping track of what the world owed him. Dad thought he was a "promising young man." Mom thought he was "extremely bright." Mary Agnes said he was a microchip.

Stanley had always been the brother I didn't have . . . the kind that if he had really *been* my brother, I'd wished I didn't have, mostly because by the time we were in high school he was every parent's idea of what a son should be. He was deviously polite, adept at any sport he wanted to try, an Eagle Scout, president of every club he ever joined and was good looking too.

Now, as juniors in high school, Amy and Mary Agnes and Stanley and I had become sort of a group—not the Wreckers of fifth grade, but a foursome that hung around together when there was nothing else to do or maybe because we amused each other. Stanley could belch anytime he wanted to. Amy could cry without once changing her expression or screwing up her face. Mary Agnes, who since fifth grade had kept telling everyone she was going to be a nun, could fold her hands and bow her head and look as if a halo and sainthood had already descended upon her. All I could do was raise one eyebrow without moving any other part of my face. It was sort of like a wordless question mark, and it drove Mom crazy.

On the way to McCray's Prairie, Stanley and I sat in the farthest seat back in Dad's new Chevy Lumina minivan, Dad and Mr. Prentice in front. I think Dad was as proud of its fancy name as he was of the new van. It had three rows of seats and tinted windows that you could look out through, but not in at. But besides cars, wildlife biology was really his passion—and his lifework. As for Stanley's dad, I think he was mostly interested in an excuse to go tramping around out-of-doors with his son after a work-week of totaling numbers and balancing budgets. Stanley said his dad viewed the entire world quantitatively.

"How do you mean?" I'd asked him.

"Graphs. Statistics. Equations. Sines. Sometimes I feel like his subtrahend."

I couldn't remember enough eighth-grade math to understand what he meant by subtrahend, but I figured Stanley was just on a downer. There was no in-between with Stanley. He was either floating on cloud nine or deep-sixing.

This morning, however, Stanley was up. Mr. Personality himself and disgustingly enthusiastic. Enthusiasm in the early morning *is* disgusting!

"Thanks to Old Dad"—he nodded toward the front seat—"they're on the trail of the perfect biome. That's what we're going out to investigate."

Long ago I had learned not to ask Stanley what a strange word meant, so I let "biomes" be "biomes" and smiled across at Stanley as if I were well aware of every species, variety, class, and phylum of biome.

"What are you doing here, Trace? How come you're not boning up for the SAT with Mary Agnes and Amy?"

"Stanley!" I punched him in the arm. "I'm being a dutiful daughter, can't you see? And incidentally, where were you last night? Your mother called. She thought you were over at our house."

"I was going to come over. Changed my mind." He

looked out the window as we turned off the highway onto a winding country road. Mary Agnes, who on the days she wasn't going to be a nun planned to be an artist, said that Stanley had a profile that belonged on a coin. It was really true, I thought, as I turned to challenge him about saying he was coming over last night. Stanley could lie convincingly—at least to his parents—and as long as I could remember, I had been his easy alibi.

"Heard your mom was on TV."

"Yeah."

I didn't offer any more information and he didn't ask. He understood how I was usually out of sync with Mom, but I couldn't understand what was missing between him and his father.

Dad parked the van on the shoulder of a gravel road and we scrambled through thick undergrowth, unmarked by paths, and there, as if purposely hidden away from intruders, was a marshy stretch of green, nestled between two hills. Red-winged blackbirds scolded from the tops of spindly cattails and two baby turtles sunning on a log splashed into the water as we approached.

"You two stay back now," Dad warned as he and Bob Prentice edged closer. Although Stanley's dad had on a T-shirt and jeans, he still looked as if he were wearing a pinstripe suit and necktie.

"Are biomes dangerous?" I asked Stanley, against my better judgment.

He didn't answer.

I spotted a tree and walked back up the hill and sat down. It was a beautiful spring day—the kind that really belongs in June but somehow pops up in the middle of April with air so gentle that you have to wet your finger and hold it up to find out where the breeze is coming from. I should have felt good, but I didn't. I guess it was the way I'd acted toward Mom—but worst of all I didn't know why I'd acted that way. It was funny. I couldn't help it. Maybe it was because watching her on TV made me feel as if we didn't belong together anymore.

"I found one!" Stanley thrust his cupped hands in front of my face.

"What?"

"A biome. Want to see it?"

"Not really."

He uncovered one hand and an ugly, crawly thing with six excited legs started up his arm.

"That's what it looks like?"

He grinned triumphantly. "I knew you didn't know what the word meant. This is a dung beetle. Do you know there are almost half a million different kinds of beetles in the world and maybe a million more that have never been identified?"

It was an old Stanley routine: start talking about something he'd read and then put it in the form of a question so that you had to listen.

"No. Somehow I never happened upon that fact." At times Stanley was completely immune to sarcasm.

"There are more beetles in the world than there are people." He scowled. "And they probably have a lot more fun."

I didn't bother to answer. Instead, I watched Dad and Stanley's father move slowly through a knee-high stretch of prairie grass beyond the marsh.

"Do you know," Stanley began again, "that if we could jump as far as fleas—in comparison to our weight, I mean—we'd be able to jump the length of two football fields? Think what that would mean to Coach Bulger and the Coolidge basketball team."

"Stanley!" I tried not to raise my voice. "Don't you ever think of more important things like how you're going to pay back the ten bucks you borrowed from Amy and me last week?"

"I haven't forgotten. It's down in The Book," he said, as if that somehow erased the debt.

As a matter of fact, it very well might have. Stanley had been keeping The Book since I was a Fifth Grade Wrecker. I'd only seen the inside of it once, and then just for a minute before he'd known I was looking and slammed it shut saying, like someone in a James Bond movie, "This is for *my* eyes only!"

What I'd seen were lists of names, including Amy's, Mary Agnes's, and mine above columns filled with little pluses and minuses and writing so tiny I couldn't read it. Probably in some sort of Stanley code. I did know, though, because he'd told me, that it was an ongoing list of who Stanley thought owed him what. When I asked him for an example he flipped a few pages, looked up at me and said, "Fifth grade. When you told everyone I'd set off the fire alarm on the way out to recess. You still owe me for that." I didn't ask again.

"You and your Book. You're sick, Stanley," I said. "Sometimes you're kind of cute but you are very, very sick. If you are not careful, you *will* grow up and you'll turn into a Certified Public Accountant just like your dad." Despite his attachment to lists and numbers, Stanley swore he was adopted.

"Stanley!" Dad shouted up from beyond the marsh.

"Come on down and bring your clipboard. We've found something special."

Stanley jogged off, and I leaned back against the tree and ate my lunch—alone. By the end of the afternoon, it had become a very long Saturday.

When we were finally in the van on the way back home, Stanley insisted on reading to me from his clipboard. "Indian grass, golden Alexander, purple coneflower, oxeye, tick trefoil . . ." He paused for a second as if waiting for me to applaud. "Black-eyed Susan, and partridge pea. Your dad says it's a practically perfect example of an ecologically balanced community. *That's* what a biome is, Trace. A self-contained unit of varied living matter. Biologically speaking, it's a home."

"I knew it all along," I said. I could usually make him furious by saying something like that.

"You did not."

"I did too. Because, *biographically* speaking, Stanley, that's what I have—a bi-home."

For once he didn't come up with an answer, and instead spent the next twenty minutes staring out the window. I finally gave up and asked what he was thinking about.

"I'm looking for visual oxymorons."

I refused to react and instead listened to my father talking about "ecological niches," "natural covers," and "transient populations." I hadn't been kidding about having a bi-home, and "transient population" fit pretty well, too, if you could apply it to a population of one.

"I think I've found what I've been looking for," Stanley announced when we pulled up in front of his house.

Even though I swore I wouldn't, I asked anyway. "Where?"

"It's me." He picked up his clipboard and climbed out. "See, there's something about an oxymoron that doesn't fit."

"Oh, come off it," I giggled. "You've always been a moron, and that fits perfectly."

Stanley didn't laugh. He looked at me in total seriousness, then turned and followed his dad.

"Come on up front, Cricket," Dad said as we drove away. "Let's get cleaned up and go out for dinner. Where would you like to eat?"

"The Carriage House." I didn't even have to think. It had always been my favorite place, and Mom and I never went there. Mostly, if we weren't going for pizzas, we ended up at Port Inn or the Elms, both of which Mom liked, but I thought were yuppie havens.

Dad raised his eyebrows. "What are we celebrating? It isn't your birthday, is it?"

For a minute Dad looked so worried that I almost laughed. As a scientist, he could remember thousands of Latin names for all sorts of plants and bugs and microbes; but he was lousy with dates. One year he missed his wedding anniversary by two months, but Mom had just laughed and said the important thing was that he hadn't forgotten they were married. That was before the repotting.

"No, that's still in March," I answered. "We're celebrating biomeness."

I didn't think he got the joke, but he grinned anyway. "Whatever you say. But I get the shower first. You're the only person in the world who takes longer in the bathroom than your mother and I'd like some dinner before it's time for breakfast."

It was fun going out to eat with Dad, partly, I had to admit, because he was honestly handsome and because he looked—well, not exactly young, but not really old enough to be a father. It was more like being on a date than being with a parent. I was wondering for the hundredth time how Mom could have let him move out of the house and into an apartment when a woman stopped at our table just as we were starting on dessert. I'd taken my first bite of the raspberry cheesecake that I shouldn't have ordered because it would probably add another pound that I didn't really need when a voice said, "Sam!" with as much delight as if *he* were a raspberry cheesecake.

Dad put down his coffee cup, stood up so fast that he practically knocked over his chair and smiled at the woman. "Chris! Won't you sit down for a minute? This is my daughter, Tracy. And Tracy, this is the newest and best addition to the university's wildlife biology department. And next semester she'll be my officemate."

She accepted the chair Dad pulled out for her. I swallowed my bite of cheesecake. I didn't like the word "officemate." "Hi," I mumbled, prepared to loathe her.

I didn't have a chance. She didn't give me one of those phony so-this-is-your-little-girl smiles. Instead, she actually looked at me as if she was really seeing me and said, "Hello, Tracy."

For the first time in my life, I understood what the word "cute" meant. Chris was 100 percent, certifiably cute and it wasn't even sickening. Her hair was so blond it was almost white, her eyes were the brightest, clearest blue I'd ever seen, her teeth were white and even, and she had what books always call a "dusting" of freckles on the bridge of her nose. All that and probably a doctorate degree, too, since she was in Dad's department.

Chris stayed more than a minute. She drank two cups of coffee, ate the last bite of my dessert which I couldn't finish, and listened with obvious interest while Dad described in detail everything Stanley had so carefully recorded from our morning trudge.

"Sounds like the ideal spot for the project." Chris was as excited as if Dad had been describing a diamond mine. "Now, if we can get started on the grant proposal next week, we should be able to wrap things up before the deadline."

Dad winked at me. "Chris is an optimist. She still thinks that grant proposals result in money. But you may be right." He turned to her. "We have the right place. We do have time. I'll get to the office early on Monday and we can begin the paperwork."

As they went on making plans, they reminded me of Mom getting ready to begin a new book. After one was finished, she'd spend months acting like a normal human being, doing the usual, everyday things a mother was supposed to do. Then, all of a sudden, just when things settled into a routine, she'd disappear behind her desk and start making lists on scraps of paper, talking to herself, tearing items out of the newspaper and acting as if nothing else in the world really existed. And that's what Chris and Dad were doing.

We finally left the Carriage House and walked across the parking lot toward the van, Dad between us, one arm draped around my shoulder as if to show everyone I belonged to him.

"It was nice meeting you, Tracy," Chris said as she unlocked the door of a sleek red Audi. "And thanks for the cheesecake. Next time maybe we can split one."

"Sure," I answered, but I wasn't sure I wanted there to be a next time.

"Well, what next?" Dad asked as we walked over to our van. "Movie?"

"There's a new horror one over at the mall." Amy and I and Mary Agnes had been dying to see it, but our allowances had never stretched that far.

The movie didn't live up to its promos. I think Dad slept through most of it. We were just walking out of the mall and had started across the street to the parking lot when a car full of kids came whizzing around the corner, brakes squealing, leaving two black marks of rubber on the pavement.

"Drunks!" Dad muttered as he grabbed my arm and pulled me back on the curb. "I ought to turn them in before they kill someone."

I didn't say anything. I couldn't. I knew my voice wouldn't work if I tried because it wasn't a drunk leaning out of the front passenger's seat. It was Stanley.

3

THE NEXT AFTERNOON WHEN DAD TOOK ME home, we found Mom out on the patio working her way through a stack of magazines that she hadn't gotten around to reading while she was writing her last book.

"What news from fields and fens?" she asked as Dad pulled up a chair and sat down.

I stopped listening when he began a less-detailed repeat of last night's conversation with Chris. Instead, I sat down and watched them—my mother and my father. It was crazy. They looked and sounded just as they always had, back before Dad moved out. They smiled at each other, made each other laugh, traded bits of information and acted as if they still lived together.

I couldn't understand why they didn't. I know they thought they'd explained everything very logically and objectively before Dad got the apartment. Dad had said things about "renewal and reevaluation" and then he'd gone on to some confusing analogy about burning off prairie grass to permit regrowth. Mom had nodded in agreement and then launched into her own explanation of the psychological and sociological implications of traditional relationships and how the real bonding of the nuclear family was a matter of commitment and not convention.

If they'd been angry or yelled at each other, it all might have made some kind of sense, but they didn't. Because of that and in spite of all their explanations, I felt like what I was: a kid being left out of adult secrets.

I spent a couple of nights crying myself to sleep until I decided maybe they were right and it wasn't a sneaky way of telling me they were getting divorced. Then I read magazine articles about putting the sizzle back in marriage, finding ways of coping with marital boredom, games married couples could play, and private time in public relations. I even took those tests they publish about "Are We Compatible?" first pretending to be Dad and then Mom. The only thing I found out was that when it came to matching up, my parents might as well have been Siamese twins.

Of course I shared all this and what was happening with Amy and Mary Agnes, but even when we began our little pep-up parties, I didn't tell them what I was really feeling because I wasn't sure myself. The biggest thing I noticed about the repotting was that Dad seemed more fun and Mom seemed more bossy.

"Right, Cricket?" Dad was looking at me, waiting for an answer, and I had no idea what he'd said. But I figured it was safe to agree, so I nodded.

Mom stared at me in amazement. "Tracy, have you become unglued? Or have you suddenly grown up?" I couldn't help but notice how beautiful her eyes were. They practically changed color with her moods. "I thought you and Amy were absolutely going to die if you didn't go to the concert."

I didn't know what I'd agreed to, but I said in my most adult tones, "There will be other concerts."

"Sam, we should have a tape of this moment." Mom was at her most dramatic. "Our beloved daughter has reached a turning point. She has become a responsible human being."

I didn't know what I was supposed to be responsible for, and I didn't much like Mom's teasing, but Dad was laughing at Mom, so I swallowed the smart-ass answer I might have given. "Speaking of being responsible," Mom said, "I almost forgot to tell you. You had three calls. One from Stanley, one from Amy, and one from the Grunt."

Dad looked at Mom. "The Grunt?"

"She's trying to be funny," I said before she could answer. "His name is Boyd and she only calls him that because he lifts weights. He's a wrestler on the varsity team." Dad placed a high priority on literacy, so I hadn't planned on mentioning Boyd to him.

"I call him the Grunt because on the phone he is almost unintelligible. He breathes more than he talks."

"Oh, Mother," I said with as much disdain as I could manage. "It just so happens that he breathes that way because his nose was broken last season."

"Have you met him yet?" Dad didn't sound impressed.

Mom clasped her hands and looked up at the sky. "So far, he's just a disembodied breath, but perhaps the inevitable is drawing near. Right, Trace?"

A couple of years ago, I would have told her all about Boyd—how he had the seat beside me in Advanced Algebra, a definite counselor error, and how he'd asked Amy, Mary Agnes, and me to come and watch him wrestle, which was *our* error. After that, he kept calling us in rotation. He never wanted anything except to talk about his diet, which was either to gain or lose weight depending on how much pizza he'd eaten over the weekend. Mom was really out of it if she thought I'd ever go out with him.

"Well, I'd better be going." Dad stood up and started toward the drive. "I'll stop by tomorrow afternoon and see if I can fix that leaky faucet."

"Oh, and Sam—the Wilsons invited us over for dinner next Wednesday. Around six-thirty."

"Okay. And Cricket. I'll make the arrangements about the overnight then."

"Sure," I said, wondering what overnight I was spending where.

Mom and I didn't go anywhere for dinner that evening; instead, we agreed to order in a pizza and then we disagreed about that. Mom wanted sausage and extra cheese. I wanted hamburger and mushrooms. Mom was paying, of course, but we compromised with a half and half.

I knew that she was beginning to think about her next book and she'd probably like to talk about it, but since it concerned daughters I didn't say anything. If she wanted to explore me, she'd have to ask. Besides, I figured she'd be writing from a mother's point of view, which was about 180 degrees from mine.

I went up to my room and closed the door, turned on the stereo and sat at my desk. I always did my best thinking when I could listen to music. It was beginning to occur to me that there were lots of things to think about. I pulled out a sheet of paper and started making a list. Mom always said that sometimes she didn't know what she was thinking until she wrote it down, and that was one thing we agreed on.

Amy. I'd call her, of course, but I'd save that until just before I went to bed.

Boyd. He probably wanted to talk about tomorrow's algebra test. I certainly didn't want a date with him, but Amy and I figured he was great for practice, so we'd be ready when someone more exciting came along. I wondered if maybe he was doing the same thing.

Mom and Dad. I stared at the words, then crossed them out. I thought of what Mom had said on TV. "There must be space in togetherness." So I wrote their names again.

Mom

Dad

They were two separate people. Maybe I was the "and" that held them together.

Speech class tomorrow. I'd die if I had to sit through the tape of Mom's TV interview. How was I going to get out of it? Muscle Man would be no help. Amy would have an idea—probably several—but she didn't answer her phone. Mary Agnes would smile weakly and say, "It's a burden you must bear for having a literate mother." I could skip speech class, but Amy and I had done that once. Once was enough!

I'd call Stanley. He always followed the rules, but he could usually find the necessary loopholes in them.

"Trace!" a frantic Stanley answered my call. "Where you been? Listen. I got to have forty bucks by homeroom tomorrow. Can you loan me some?"

"How much is some?"

"Forty dollars?"

He knew I had that much left from my birthday money, the pig!

"I'll pay you back. Honest. With interest."

"How much?"

"Ten percent."

I don't know why I didn't ask him what he wanted the money for, but Stanley was Stanley and I was sure he was smart enough to know what he was doing.

"I'll bring it in the morning."

I finally gave up on how I was going to weasel out of speech class and turned off the light. Thinking obviously didn't help, nor did making lists. I'd just wait until tomorrow and play it by ear. Besides, who knew what might happen. As Mary Agnes always said, "Tomorrow might never come."

Tomorrow came, and it was a definite Monday. First, I couldn't find the jeans I wanted to wear and then I remembered Mom had worn them for the interview and they were still in the laundry and it had been my turn to do it and I hadn't. My hair was a mess. It had somehow developed a cowlick during the night, and no amount of brushing could make it lie flat. And there wasn't time to wash it because I was already ten minutes late, which meant I couldn't walk to school with Amy because she had a student council meeting before school on Mondays.

I got to school just before the bell for homeroom and just in time to run into Boyd in the hall. He had been waiting for me, I was sure. I had to admit he was kind of cute in a beefy way and had the biggest biceps of anyone on the team. His pectorals weren't bad, either.

"How come you didn't call me back?" he asked. Mom was right. He did sort of grunt out some of his words. "I

. . . waited up . . . until nine-thirty. That's Coach's curfew."

"Mom forgot to tell me," I lied quickly. "I just found the note this morning. What did you want?"

"I couldn't get that sixth problem. You know, the one about Tina." He fumbled in his notebook. "In five years Tina will be twice the age she was three years ago. How old is she now?"

"Boyd, be a good boy and forget about Tina. I have problems of my own." I considered asking him if there was a place I could hide down in the gym, under a wrestling mat, maybe.

"But Trace. I have to get at least one right. If I flunk again I won't be eligible next year." As he talked he moved his shoulders in aerobic circles that caused his chest to expand and his neck to disappear into his collarbone. "What's your problem, babe?"

"Jackson's speech class."

"Canceled." He was exercising his left fist now, opening and shutting it as he counted.

"Who said?"

"Announced it in homeroom last Friday. Don't you remember? All this week, Jackson's giving a crash course on how to pass the SAT."

I was saved! I could have hugged him, but he was inhaling a deep breath—through his mouth. "I'm learning to belly-breathe," he explained between gulps of air. I waited until he had finished his ten wheezes, and we walked into homeroom.

An anxious Stanley was waiting for me.

"Thanks, Trace," he mumbled as he pocketed the forty dollars. "I'll put it down in The Book."

"Is something wrong? I mean, you sounded so weird over the phone," I said, wondering if I should tell him I had another twenty-five dollars stashed away if he really needed it.

"Nothing that I can't handle."

Knowing Stanley, I was certain he could, but after the first day of Jackson's crash course, I wasn't sure I could handle the SAT. For as long as I could remember, they'd been getting us ready for whatever was coming next. "You must learn these things so you'll be prepared for junior high school." In junior high it was "so you'll be ready for high school." In high school, now, it was "so you'll be ready for college." Wasn't there ever a now? Throughout the grades we'd been aptituded, preferentialed, basic-skilled, readied, normed, graphed, and IQ-ed every other year or so. DAT. COPS. CTBS. I'd had them all. I'd often wondered how many thousands of little blank circles I'd filled in with my newly sharpened number two pencil during my lifetime. But the SAT was the biggie. The dreaded Scholastic Aptitude Test. The name alone was enough to scare anyone.

"The SAT on Saturday," Amy reminded me. "Isn't it fitting? SAT on Sat."

Amy, of course, didn't worry about the test, but my life depended on it. I had to prove to Dad that I was as smart as he thought I was and I had to make Mom believe I was just as smart as she; but besides, I had to score high so I could send in my application to a college in California that I'd picked out. Mom, of course, wasn't too excited about that.

"It's so far away."

"I know."

"You won't be able to come home except for Christmas."

"I know."

"What's wrong with a small college here in the Middle West?"

"Everything. Like what you said in one of your books: 'Esthetic enjoyment creates intellectual energy.' "

Mom didn't have an answer to that.

I had found my college after hours in the counselor's office, poring through catalogues.

> *We want people who recognize a responsibility to society and a commitment to service. We want people who are committed to learning.*

After reading that, I wasn't too sure that was the college for me, but it was the lush greenness of the palm trees, the expanse of tennis courts, students surfing and lying around on beaches that convinced me.

"I could major in marine biology, Mom." My SAT scores had to look good.

Amy and I had flunked our first important educational test-out, a standardized test of basic skills. We were in grade school—fourth grade, maybe. I'd started to answer the questions in the test booklet and to fill in the circles on my answer sheet when I looked over at Amy.

"Dumb!" she whispered.

She wasn't answering the questions. She wasn't even reading them. She was making little designs of the circles on her answer sheet. I turned back to my test and read:

A CAT IS TO A KITTEN AS A ________ IS TO A COLT.

a. DOG
b. HORSE
c. CHICKEN
d. FISH

I had to agree. The questions were dumb. So I made diagonal lines of the circles down the page, just like Amy: triangles, Xs, squares, Ls, and lopsided boxes that turned into steps leading down and disappearing off the lower-right-hand corner of my page.

We both learned—after a week in detention—the fundamental truth of our education: to learn was to be tested—often!

SATs are so important they don't even trust your own high school teachers to administer them. Instead, we all had to register ahead of time, pay money and appear at the university. On a Saturday, yet! Mary Agnes picked us up, Stanley, Amy, and me, early that morning and drove us across town to the university. Mary Agnes was always our designated driver since she had her own car and she was the kind of person every mother trusted.

"Did you all bring your number two pencils?" Mary Agnes chirped from the driver's seat.

"Wouldn't you know," groaned Amy. "I thought about it last night and forgot. Stanley, do you have an extra one?"

"Need you ask?" Mary Agnes smiled up at the rearview mirror and winked at Stanley.

"I brought along a box. They're sharpened."

I think that's why we included Stanley. If Mary Agnes was trustworthy, Stanley was boringly reliable.

"I suppose you spent last night boning up for this." Amy turned around to Stanley.

"Not really." He looked out the window. "The guide said to spend the evening relaxing. I did."

"What did you do?" But before Stanley had a chance to answer, Mary Agnes zoomed into a parking lot right next to Wentworth Hall, where the tests were to be given.

"You can't park here!" I shouted. "It's marked Reserved. B Permit Required!"

"Who said?"

"The sign said."

"Didn't see it."

We started toward the hall, Stanley following two steps behind us. "If someone asks us what we did over the weekend, we can say we sat for the SAT."

It was a typical Stanley funny, so we purposely refused to laugh, but somehow we lost Stanley shortly after we walked up the steps to the main entrance.

"I think Stanley's scared," Amy remarked. "Did you see how jittery he was?"

"I didn't notice," I replied, as we entered the auditorium.

The room was too large to think in. Didn't they know people had to be nooked or cozied into a corner to concentrate? Why else did the monks of the Middle Ages study in tiny, dark cells rather than in shiny, slick halls flooded by fluorescents swinging down from high ceilings upon rows and rows of tables and chairs.

The three of us found a table and sat down. I couldn't see anyone I knew, and all the strange kids looked so assured and brilliant I was positive I'd draw a blank on printing my name. Maybe I didn't want to apply to a

California college. Maybe I didn't want to go to college—ever.

Someone finally slapped a test booklet in front of me, and a disembodied voice from somewhere announced, "Be sure you are using a number two pencil. Do not open your test booklet until you hear the signal to do so. You will discover that the SAT and the TSWE are in the same test booklet."

"What's the TSWE?" I whispered across to Mary Agnes.

"I don't know. Just wing it!"

"There are six sections in your test booklet. You will be given thirty minutes to work on each section, and you are expected to remain here in the testing room until all six sections have been completed."

"Three hours?" I gasped.

"You may now open your test booklets and begin."

Pages fluttered, and I was awash in antonyms, analogies, sentence completions, mathematical conundrums, and TSWE, which turned out to be another test, of course, Test of Standard Written English. The first few questions of each section were easy; then they got harder; then easier, then harder so that after the first thirty minutes I felt as if I were floundering in a pool of words with someone pushing me under then pulling me up and pushing me under and pulling me up.

"Gross!" Mary Agnes sighed.

"Sadistic!" Amy muttered.

By the time I got to the TSWE, the little flattened circles on my answer sheet looked like blank fish eyes, and I wasn't caring whether my written English was standard or not. Was it "edge of the water" or "water's edge"? If I guessed wrong, it would cost me a fraction of a minus point against my score, but if I skipped the "water's edge" or the "edge of the water" or whatever, it wouldn't count against me quite as much. At least that's what the Official Guide to the SAT had maintained, only it hadn't said anything about "water's edge." The trouble was I'd already skipped too many questions to risk not answering another one.

Mary Agnes kept sighing every time she filled in an answer, and the guy next to her was continually sniffing and wiping his nose without a handkerchief, and I was stuck on the "water's edge."

My back ached and one leg felt like a pincushion full of pins. Thirty minutes and six sections! Three hours! It was beginning to feel like six. "Water's edge" or "edge of the water"? To think my future might depend upon an apostrophe. I closed my eyes. I could see the water lapping against the shore making a distinctive line that moved like a snake between the lake and the sand. Why was it the "water's edge"? Why not the "shore's edge" or the "edge of the shore"?

"The apostrophe shows possession." I could hear Miss Rutherford in eighth-grade grammar class. That was it! It was "water's edge" because the water, not the shore, *owned* the edge. It made sense.

But on the other hand . . .

With a shrug, I filled in the blank fish eye on my answer sheet for "edge of the water." It took more words, but it sounded more mysterious, more threatening, more distant. With "water's edge" you were already at the edge, but with "edge of the water" you were standing back, wondering if you'd dare.

One thing you can say about time. If you wait long enough, it passes. Eventually the Voice from on High announced, "Time's up!"

"Inhuman!" Amy moaned as we escaped out-of-doors.

"Positively gruesome," Mary Agnes added. "But where was Stanley? I didn't see him in there, did you?"

"I wasn't looking," Amy said. "After that math section, I couldn't have seen him if he'd been standing in front of me."

Come to think about Stanley—and I didn't think about Stanley any more than I had to—I hadn't seen him since he left us on the front steps. "He'll probably meet us in the parking lot."

"Yeah," Amy laughed, "along with the campus police and your parking ticket."

We didn't see the police or the parking ticket, but we did see Stanley, sitting nonchalantly in the back seat.

"How'd you get out here so fast?" Mary Agnes pulled open the car door.

"I didn't go in." He grinned a perfectly insipid grin.

"Stanley!" I sounded just like Mom. "You mean you didn't take the test?"

"The test wasn't that bad, you dork." Mary Agnes was still holding the car door open, as if she expected Stanley to get out and explain.

"What'll your folks say?" It was a dumb question. I knew without asking what they'd say. "I mean, what are you going to tell them?"

"I'm not going to tell them." He wasn't sounding at all like Stanley.

"Why?" I climbed in the back seat beside him. "When you were registered and all. . . ."

"I didn't feel like it. I'll take it some other time."

None of us had an answer or another question to that. Mary Agnes and Amy got into the front seat and we took off.

"At least we didn't get a parking ticket," Mary Agnes gloated. "If you three would just learn to trust me."

"You did get a ticket." Stanley grinned. In fact he hadn't stopped grinning. "I tore it up."

Mary Agnes laughed. Amy looked back over her shoulder and rolled her eyes. I looked across at Stanley. For someone who still had the SAT to face, he seemed to be feeling awfully good.

4

AFTER AN EXCRUCIATING WEEK AT SCHOOL that included two whole periods of speech class spent on Welda Spencer—one for watching the interview itself and the other for discussion during which I pretended to have a combination of deafness and laryngitis—I was ready for something different.

One of the few things that Mom hadn't objected to lately was my staying overnight with Amy. I wasn't sure if that was because she truly believed Amy was a good influence—"She's so polite. . . . She doesn't mumble. . . . She always picks up after herself"—or because Mom was "fond"—her word—of Mrs. Thornton. "So genuine! She knows how to cope. When I get to *T,* it'll be *Help Yourself with Twins.*"

Partly to soften Mom up, just in case, and mostly because it was my turn, I cleared the dinner table and put stuff in the dishwasher while Mom had her last cup of coffee for the day.

"It says here"—Mom pointed at the evening newspaper—"that sixty percent of sixteen-year-olds have had some sort of sexual experience. Can you believe that?" She looked up at me over the top of her half-glasses, glasses that I doubted she needed. I was sure she wore them because she knew she looked kind of cute with them on.

I thought of my class at Calvin Coolidge High School. "No." I saw Mom kind of relax until I added, "Make that ninety-eight percent."

I wasn't exactly kidding, if what most of the girls I knew said was true. Of course, none of them came right out with details, but besides Amy and Mary Agnes and me, I didn't know anybody who'd deny it.

Mom took off her glasses, laid them on the table and then picked them up again as if she didn't know where they came from. "You mean, Tracy, all your friends . . . ?"

"Oh, Mom! In the first place, I don't have that many friends. And in the second place, this is *now.* It's not like it was back when you were a kid."

The minute I said that, I knew I'd made a mistake and was probably in for a half-hour lecture on promiscuity or, as Mary Agnes said, "promise-cutie."

"You're right."

I couldn't believe my ears!

"It's not what it was like at all." She stared past me as if she were looking at something very far away. "It's funny, but when I was your age, I didn't think there was anything to be afraid of. It wasn't until after you were born that I began to worry about the dangers in the world."

"Dangers?" I sat down at the table with her. It was hard to connect that word with my in-control mother. "You mean bombs, hijackers, terrorists?"

"No. No, those are unnatural disasters. I mean everyday things like hot stoves, sharp knives, scissors, cars that don't stop at stop signs. You were so little. So . . . vulnerable."

"Not any more. I've grown up, or haven't you noticed?"

"Growing, growing, gone," Mom said softly. Then she laughed. "Or maybe it's groan, groan, and gone."

I wasn't sure she was joking, but I laughed anyway. "Is it okay if I *do* go? To Amy's, I mean, tomorrow night and stay over?"

"You could ask her over here, you know. Her mother has her hands full with those twins. Does she know that Amy's invited you?"

Amy hadn't invited me. That was something little kids did when they had slumber parties and belonged to the Brownies. Sometimes Mom was totally out of it.

"Sure," I lied. "We'll probably be twin-sitting." I knew that would clinch it. Mom was always telling me that I needed to be more responsible, and to her, taking care of the twins showed maximum responsibility.

When I called Amy to tell her I'd be over around seven to stay all night, she practically broke my right eardrum.

"Terrific!" she shouted. "I was going to call you. I just talked to Mary Agnes and you can't guess what we're going to do."

"Go for a walk and count manhole covers?" Our art teacher had told us that was one way to appreciate design in relation to utility.

"No, you dipstick! They're having a beer blast out at Zumwalt Station, and I told my mother I was going to stay overnight with you. You know what she asked me?"

"Can't imagine."

" 'Does Tracy's mother know that Tracy invited you?' "

We both laughed. Our mothers were sometimes hopelessly outdated.

"So we're home free?" I asked. "Let me get this straight. Your mother thinks you're staying here and my mom thinks I'm staying with you. But you'd better tell your mother that we'll spend the evening here and sleep at your place."

"Got it."

The next evening, Amy and I met on a street corner halfway between her house and mine and waited for Mary Agnes to pick us up. We didn't have to wait long. Mary Agnes was a stickler for promptness.

"All aboard," she called as we climbed in. "Next stop Zumwalt Station and some cold fizzy."

"Don't forget you're the designated driver, Mary Agnes," Amy warned. "You can't have too many."

"You don't have to worry. Stanley figured it all out for me. According to my weight, I can consume one beer per hour and still be under the legal limit."

"It's different, though, isn't it, with different people?" I asked. "Some can and some can't."

"Don't worry. We aren't going to get squashed." Mary Agnes whipped off the highway onto a gravel road. "We'll just do a little social sipping. I hear some of the football team are going to be there. You know. Jeff and Brent and guys like that."

"Since when have we become football fans?" I poked Amy. "You've never been able to tell your right end from your left end."

"We have been fans since we found out that they are

supplying the kegs. All we have to do is admire their beautiful bodies and try to remember the words to the football fight song."

"Aren't those guys supposed to be in training? Coach will make them run laps for the next three years if he finds out."

"Duty is only skin-deep," Mary Agnes answered. "Besides, it's a fact of life—coaches, like real human beings, see only what they expect to see. Take me, for example."

"No way!" Amy and I shouted in unison.

She ignored us and went on. "All I had to do was suggest in fifth grade that I heard a convent calling. Did anyone except my parents remember we were Presbyterians?"

"No way!" Amy and I shouted again.

"Well," she said, "what I'm trying to say is the pie is in the eye of the beholder."

"Mary Agnes." Amy reached over and touched her forehead. "Are you sure you're totally with us? If you're going to be our senior-class president next year, you'd better switch channels."

We skidded and bumped over the gravel road that dwindled into a dirt lane. The unused railroad tracks, overgrown by weeds, were the only evidence that trains had ever stopped here, except for the station itself.

"End of the line," Mary Agnes announced as we pulled into a grove of trees that fringed a parking lot half filled with cars.

Zumwalt Station was a Calvin Coolidge High School legend because generations of students used it for beer blasts when the weather was warm enough and when it wasn't taken over by kids from the university. The building was still there, and music was blaring from inside. I couldn't decide whether it looked inviting or forbidding.

"How come we're doing this?" I asked, trying to be heard over the music.

"Because we're not supposed to, naturally," Amy yelled in my ear.

"Otherwise, it's terminal Saturday-night boredom," Mary Agnes bellowed. "Upward and onward."

As we walked nearer, I could see someone standing like a sentinel by the door. "They can't be checking for IDs, can they?" I had a driver's license, but the date on it wouldn't even get me into an adult movie.

"Don't be silly," Amy said. "They might be selling phony ones, but they sure aren't checking."

Mary Agnes didn't hesitate; she strode on, three or four steps ahead of us.

"Stanley!" she shouted, sounding like an audio rerun of my mother. "What are you doing here by yourself?"

Stanley looked at Mary Agnes and then at Amy and me. "I'm not by myself. You're all here." He leaned back against the doorjamb. "Before we were all here . . . I was there." He motioned toward the woods. "Camping out." He smiled at us, teetered for a split second and fell forward, flat in the grass.

We all leaned over and stared down at him.

"Stop playing dead!" I shouted.

I was so angry that I could have killed him deader than he looked. He'd faked this once before, when we were kids, and I had believed him. He'd found an acorn in our back yard. "It brings good luck," he told me, "but if you crack it and eat it, you die instantly."

I dared him to crack it open. He pounded until he

extracted a sliver of pulp from the broken shell, grinned at me and stuck it in his mouth. After he made a big deal of chewing it, he crossed his eyes and fell over sideways. I'd screamed for Mom, who gave Stanley a swat on his behind that brought him back to life and gave me a hug and a kiss that made me feel a little less stupid.

I almost wished Mom would appear right now, but I knew she couldn't materialize from the darkness. The three of us waited for Stanley to get up or at least move. He didn't. It was Mary Agnes who finally knelt beside him and shook his shoulders, then patted him hard on the face.

"Is he sick?" I asked.

"Is he alive?" Amy sounded frightened.

"He's had too much to drink," Mary Agnes said. "As a matter of fact, he's passed out."

"What should we do?" There had to be some kind of crazy mistake. Stanley, the brain . . . Stanley, the model student . . . Stanley, the careful list maker whom I'd known since kindergarten couldn't be lying there drunk in the grass.

"We could let him sleep. He'll wake up sooner or later." Mary Agnes stood up and looked around. "Oh . . . but . . ." She pointed out across the flat cornfield.

A mile or so away a car, its red light flashing, moved toward us.

"Cops!" I could hardly recognize it as Amy's voice.

"We've got to get out of here," Mary Agnes shouted. "Run!"

"What about Stanley?" I grabbed her arm. "We can't leave him here. He's drunk! And he's not old enough to be drunk."

Stanley still had not moved.

"He's not only drunk, Trace. He's stoned. Can't you smell the pot?" Mary Agnes looked around frantically.

"What are we going to do?" I tried not to scream.

Amy hadn't moved either, nor had she said anything. All she had done was stare down at the lifeless Stanley. "Grab his legs," she finally suggested. "We'll drag him over to the woods. Maybe we can find his tent."

"What if they take down license numbers on all the cars?" I gasped as I draped one limp Stanley arm around my shoulder. Mary Agnes did the same, while Amy grabbed his legs.

"Quit what-iffing and keep moving," Amy sputtered. The flashing lights were drawing nearer now as the police car swept into the dirt lane.

"If I get out of this . . ." Mary Agnes began, and then ran out of breath.

Just before the police car pulled up in front of the station, I caught sight of a lone tent pitched by a grove of trees that edged a ravine.

"This must be it." Amy still hadn't gotten her natural voice back yet. Mary Agnes and I propped Stanley against a tree and sat down, exhausted. Amy peeked into the tent. "He's here by himself."

"We can't leave him, then," I cried.

"Don't forget, I have to get my car out of there." Mary Agnes ran both hands through her hair.

"Listen." Amy turned to Mary Agnes. "You go on home. Don't turn your car lights on until you're out on the gravel road. Trace and I will stay here until Stanley decides to join the living again."

"How will you two get home?"

"Walk." Amy gave Mary Agnes a push. "Get going,

now, before they call in a whole posse of G-men to take down license numbers."

"But it's three miles!" I couldn't believe what I was hearing.

"So?" I could feel Amy's glare even though it was too dark to see it. "Get going, Mary Agnes."

Mary Agnes took off across the field, and I went over and sat down beside Stanley. His hand felt cold. I put my hand on his forehead. It was cold too, and damp with sweat.

"Ooooo," he groaned, and tried to raise one arm.

I drew in a deep breath. I hadn't realized I had almost quit breathing for the last several minutes.

"Stanley, you creep! You *are* alive." Amy sounded almost disappointed.

He opened his eyes, looked at us blankly and closed them again. "Sleepy," he mumbled. "Got to . . . get some shut-eye."

"So what do we do now? Should we make him throw up or something?" None of the techniques we'd learned in first-aid class applied to this. Poison, yes; too much beer, no.

"Yuuck! You mean stick *our* fingers down *his* throat? No way. He drank the stuff, let him get rid of it." She leaned against the tree and stuck her hands in her jeans pockets.

"It sure doesn't look like much fun, does it." I nudged Stanley with my foot. He didn't move. "The last time I was that sick, I was five years old and pigged out on candy corn and M&M's."

"It's not quite the same thing, Trace. But you know what? He owes us one. A big one. If it weren't for us, they'd have picked him up." She gestured toward the station, where two police cars now sat, cherry lights blinking. "His parents would have killed him."

"If they didn't drop dead of shock first. To them, Stanley is Mr. Perfect. You know everything about everybody—how come you never told me he was a party animal?"

"I didn't know he was. Besides, this doesn't exactly qualify as a party, does it?" She pointed at the tent with its solitary sleeping bag. "Listen, we'd better head home. How long does it take to walk three miles?"

"I'm not sure, but it'll be easier if you think of it as three times around South Ridge Mall." I felt a little guilty about leaving Stanley to sleep it off, but the evening was warm, so at least he wouldn't catch pneumonia.

For the first mile, Amy and I didn't talk. It was a perfect spring evening, a sky full of stars and the sounds of peepers calling from the low, damp places in the fields. It didn't seem very important that we'd missed the beer blast. The sight of Stanley falling face forward in the grass had taken an edge off any possible fun.

By the middle of the second mile, Amy's steps were slower and she was making little puffing sounds and slapping at the early mosquitoes.

"Just pretend it's a very large shopping mall," I reminded her, happy that I hadn't decided to wear sandals.

"Shopping malls are hygienic," she said through what I knew were gritted teeth. "They don't have bugs. The floors are smooth and they smell good." We were passing a feed lot full of cattle, lined up in a black mass against the barbed-wire fence. There was something silent and menacing in their bulkiness. Both of us walked faster.

We finally reached the outskirts of town and took off our shoes, our bare feet splatting softly on the cement sidewalk. Neither one of us was talking now. We turned down Amy's street. Lights were on in the house, the porch light was ablaze, and the patio spotlight shone down on Amy's mom and my mom.

Amy stopped. "What are we going to tell them?"

"We can't tell them the truth. Stanley would be incarcerated for years."

"We can tell them part of the truth," Amy suggested.

"Which part?"

"That we were riding around with Mary Agnes and . . ."

"We had a flat tire?" I added.

"I said tell them part of the truth—not make up the truth. We went riding around with Mary Agnes and it was such a nice night we decided to walk home just for fun."

"The outdoor air must have disintegrated your brain. Who's going to believe that you would put one foot in front of the other unless you were shopping?"

"No good?" Amy asked.

"It stinks," I said.

"How about Mary Agnes absolutely had to be home at ten o'clock so we offered to walk over from her house. And straighten up and walk fast so we'll look as if we've just walked a few blocks."

We picked up the pace and practically jogged over to the patio.

"Hi!" Amy sang out.

"Mom," I exclaimed in faked surprise.

It was not a convincing introduction to what we were

trying to pawn off as the cross-your-heart truth.

Mom jumped up from her lawn chair. "*Where* have you been?" There was a definite accent on the "where." "Gretchen and I have been frantic, worrying over you two."

Amy's mom didn't look too frantic to me, stretched out in her nightdress on the chaise longue, her bare feet dangling over the end.

"We were with Mary Agnes." Amy collapsed on the patio bench. "We went riding."

"And she had to be home at ten, so we said we'd walk from her house so she wouldn't be late." I sat down on the bottom step and massaged my sore foot.

"Mary Agnes . . ." Mom sank back down in her chair. "Well . . ." Mom was not often caught speechless. "I guess we shouldn't have worried if you were with Mary Agnes. The trouble was Gretchen thought you two were staying at our house, and I thought you were staying at her house."

"We changed our minds." Amy smiled across at Mom. "We were going to stay at your house, only Trace said she'd have to change her sheets. I changed mine this morning, so we decided to stay here." Amy glanced over at me and shrugged her shoulders as if to say, "See? See how it's done?"

Later, after Mom had left and Amy and I had gone to bed and turned off the lights, I heard Amy giggling.

"What's so funny?" After all, we'd been lucky not to have been picked up by the cops, we'd plodded three miles over gravel roads, and we'd almost been in major trouble with our parents.

"Mothers!"

I heard the sheets rustle and knew Amy was sitting up in bed, which meant at least an hour of late-night talk. In the mornings, until at least ten, she usually functioned like a zombie, but something about nighttime pushed her discussion button. She would have made a superior vampire.

"What about them?" There had been nothing even vaguely amusing about Mom's greeting earlier.

"They're so suspicious. They always think of the absolutely worst thing that could possibly happen, like your Mom, or they can't believe we'd have enough originality to do anything potentially depraved—like mine."

I thought about that for a minute. "Yeah, and they're so naive. All we had to do was mention Mary Agnes. Maybe it's a good thing that they've forgotten what it's like to be sixteen."

"Maybe they never were sixteen. My mother, I mean. I think she went from being born to having babies without anything in between. At least your mom has some imagination. Too bad she didn't pass it on to you." She threw her pillow and caught me by surprise.

I tossed it back. I thought Amy's mom was really nifty; nothing ever seemed to bother her. She was a big, warm, soft kind of person who never tried to be cute or funny. Most of all, ever since I'd known her, she'd never changed, even after the twins were born.

"Yes," I finally said, "but yours doesn't spend Saturday evening on the telephone checking up to see if you're where you said you were going to be."

"That's better than being totally out of it. I could probably be pushing crack, and Mom would think it was a Girl Scout project." I heard her lie down in her twin bed and pull the sheets around her. She hadn't changed the sheets.

"I hope Stanley's all right," she said softly.

"I do, too," I agreed.

"He could have died, you know."

I didn't know.

5

THE NEXT WEEK, SCHOOL BEGAN RELAtively calmly for Calvin Coolidge High: no food fights, no one dangling someone else out a third-floor window, no one trying to make videotapes of the girls' locker room. Mary Agnes had evaded the police on the way home and was looking more saintly than ever with her prim smile and ladylike voice. Stanley was his normal punctual, list-making self, this time collecting names of kids who'd be ushers for graduation. When Amy and I tried to tease him about his out-of-body experience, he looked as blank as he had that night. I wasn't sure whether he was pretending or if he really didn't remember our dragging him across the pasture.

The surprise of my week, however, came Tuesday night when Mom tossed a pair of plane tickets on the dinner table and said, "Only one carry-on bag, Tracy. You promised. Remember?"

I hadn't forgotten. I'd just pushed the coming weekend out of my mind. Mother's Day wasn't my idea of a national holiday, but I couldn't very well say that. I knew we were flying to Arizona to see my grandmother, and this year it was Grandma Ida's birthday on that weekend.

"Sure," I answered. "I won't need many clothes. It's sort of a retirement home, isn't it? Nobody's going to notice what I look like."

Mom smiled at me, a little too sweetly. "Don't be so sure. I think my mother has gone from bluebirds to bridge. The community isn't exactly senile."

Mom and Dad had helped Grandma move out there, a little over a year ago. After Grandpa died, she'd tried to live by herself on the farm, but one day she announced she was going to move to Arizona into "one of those condos where someone else takes care of my house and my yard and my flowers." Her friend Bertha told Mom, "Your mother's been watching too many of those TV talk shows that tell you how *not* to be old when you *are.*" Grandma said that wasn't true—that she just wanted to see if she still had the "gumption to change" after all her years of being a farm wife.

Grandma usually called at least once a month or else Mom called her and I usually talked for a couple of minutes, but she would get so busy asking about what *I* was doing that she never said much about her own life.

That Friday, by the time Mom and I were on our way to Arizona, sitting belted in side by side, I was convinced that no mother and daughter should ever travel any place together.

"Don't you think you should have worn something different than that sweatshirt and shorts? Did you have any longer shorts clean rather than those short shorts?"

"Who's looking?" I grumped, clamping the headset over my ears and switching to the rock channel.

Mom was wearing her Banana Republic jumpsuit that she wore when she was on the book-tour circuit. She could have passed for the Wynonna half of the Judds.

Mom touched my arm. Her lips were moving, but I couldn't hear what she was saying.

"What?" I yanked off the headset.

"I said did you remember to take out the garbage?"

"Yes, Mother. I took out the garbage."

"And you *did* lock the back door."

"Yes. I locked the back door."

"I wonder if I disconnected my word processor. You know, in case it storms. If lightning strikes and the electricity goes off I'll lose everything I have on SAVE."

"Cool it, Mom." I slipped the headset back on. "Everyone is looking at us." They weren't, but I felt as if they were. Mom had a voice that carried. I took out the flight magazine and started thumbing through it, looking at the pictures and pretending to read.

Mom elbowed me gently in the ribs. I took off the headset and switched off the music.

"Would you mind, Tracy, trading places with me, since you're going to read? I'd like to sit next to the window."

"Sure." I tucked the earphones into the pocket in the back of the seat ahead of me.

"Pardon us." Mom smiled at the man in the aisle seat. "We're going to trade seats. My daughter wants to read and I want to look out at the clouds."

The man smiled and stepped out into the aisle, blocking the drink cart from getting through. Mom stepped out. I stepped out. Mom stepped in. I stepped in, and the man settled down beside me, his left arm at least six inches over into my space. No wonder Mom wanted to trade seats.

It was at least fifteen minutes before the drink cart got back to us. Mom insisted on sitting in the tail of the plane. Somewhere she'd read it was the safest place. She took forever to answer the simple question, "Would you like something to drink?" and then asked for apple juice, which, of course, the stewardess didn't have.

When we were finally in the landing pattern for Phoenix, I even had to remind her to straighten her seat to the upright position that the flight attendants demanded. It didn't help that when we stopped at the gate the man beside me practically did contortions to get her luggage out of the overhead bin and ignored my backpack which was stashed right beside it.

Mom refused to move until almost everyone else was off the plane, and then she said as we started up the aisle, "Wasn't that fun, Tracy? I never get tired of flying. It always seems like such an impossibility."

"It is an impossibility," I muttered, but she didn't hear me because the flight attendants were saying good-bye to her as if they were old friends. People often reacted that way toward her. I couldn't figure out why.

By the time we got to the gate, most of the other passengers were on their way to pick up luggage. My grandmother stood alone, waiting for us.

The woman I remembered had been small and wrinkled, her hair carelessly cut and her clothes as casual as the short shorts I was wearing. Her passion had been bluebirds, and she'd spent most of her time putting up nesting boxes or cleaning them out all over the farm where she'd lived the whole time I was growing up.

"Dotty! And dear Tracy!"

Only Grandma Ida called Mom Dotty.

The woman who opened her arms to us seemed taller. Her silk pants suit was spotless, and her haircut would have made Amy rush to the mall for a copy. When she hugged me, I was enveloped in a lovely haze of expensive perfume—Giorgio, I thought, though I'd only smelled it on those tear-out strips in one of Mom's magazines.

"My two girls," she said. "How wonderful that you would come." She hugged Mom again. "I didn't know how much I'd missed you until I saw you." I never noticed before that they looked alike; even their voices sounded the same.

They walked on ahead of me, their arms entwined, and I followed, feeling like the third leg of a tripod.

"I thought we'd stop for dinner. . . ." Grandma looked at my torn sweatshirt and short shorts. "But perhaps we should stop off at the condo and . . . freshen up."

She didn't say so I could change my clothes, but I knew that's what she was thinking. I had to admit, she and Mom looked like something out of a fashion magazine and I was obviously Salvation Army salvage.

When we reached Grandma's condo, Mom took one look, fell back into the nearest chair and said, "Let's not go out. Let's eat here, and I know very well, Ida, you have a refrigerator full of goodies."

My mother grew up calling her mother by her first name, and later, as I watched their synchronized movements about the tiny all-white kitchen, they acted more like girlfriends than mother and daughter.

By the time I was ready for bed, I was in semi-shock. There was nothing grandmotherly about the condo. Instead of the overstuffed furniture and the frilly lampshades and rows of family photos in engraved frames that I remembered from the farm, the place was sleek and bare, its whiteness accented with a couple of vivid Navaho rugs and pieces of Indian pottery.

"Grandma," I finally said, while Mom was putting stuff in the dishwasher, "I like your place, but it's so different from your house on the farm."

"I know. It's supposed to be." She repositioned a chair that Mom had moved. "The lady who helped me decorate said I should keep that chair there by the window because its colors will tend to pull the outdoors into the room. They're big on outdoors out here. You see, Tracy"—she sat down beside me, in a matching chair—"after your grandpa died, I vowed I would never let myself become a burden or a bother to your mother. So I had to prove to myself that I was brave enough to get out on my own—to try something new—to see if I could still grow and change. What is it you say now? Do my own thing. And this"—she gestured around the room—"seemed the best way to do it. Does that make sense?"

"Of course," I answered. "Mom could probably make a new book about it: *Help Yourself with Condominiums.*" Before I could stop myself, I started to yawn. "I'm getting sleepy."

"Of course you are, honey." She took my hand and pulled me out of my chair. "It's time for all of us to be in bed."

As I followed her out of the living room, I decided that despite the new outside, Grandma was alive and well and hadn't changed all that much after all. "This will be your room, Tracy," she said. "You'd probably like a little privacy. Your mother and I will share my room. Sleep as late as you want in the morning." When she kissed me good night, it almost made up for the plane ride. I kissed her back and wondered when it was that Mom and I had stopped doing that.

Once, very late that night or very early in the morning, I woke to the sound of laughter coming from across the hall. At first, I didn't know where I was, and then I realized it was Mom and Grandma Ida. They were pulling an all-nighter.

The next morning, early, Grandma—I couldn't make myself call her Ida—took us on a tour of her complex: the rec hall, the saunas, the hot tubs, the pools, the exercise room. The whole place was so void of kids and clutter that I felt like an intruder. As we walked around the grounds, I would have welcomed even a discarded gum wrapper to disfigure the tiresome, green perfection of the lawns. It was a strange place, nothing moving—no cars or people or time—until about ten-thirty.

We were sitting in the shade of an umbrella at the edge of a huge but empty swimming pool when the population exploded. One minute there was no one around, the next minute there were people everywhere, looking tanned and energetic and healthy—all of them my grandmother's age or older.

Mom was as surprised as I. "Where did they come from, Ida?"

Grandma laughed. "I know what you mean. It took me over a month to catch on to the schedule. The tennis players and the golfers are up and playing by seven and they get back about now. The swimmers and sunners emerge next, then the bridge players, and, about five, the parties begin. Most people go to dinner around eight." Her voice drifted off.

Mom leaned forward and I thought she was going to ask a question, but for the next half hour she didn't have a chance because people kept stopping by to say hello—all old people, trying to *be* again what they'd been.

"Good morning, Ida." A woman in a bathing suit, black hair falling down to her shoulders, sauntered by on the arm of a gray-mustached man. From the back she might have been a high school cheerleader. "Remember, it's duplicate bridge this afternoon."

"I'll be there," Grandma called after them.

"Ida! There you are." The woman was so thin that her head looked too big for her body. I could almost hear Mary Agnes hissing "anorexic." Amy would have killed for the jogging suit. It had obviously not been intended for anything as ordinary as exercise. Grandma introduced her as "president of the board of our condominium complex—Alicia Halston."

The woman perched on the arm of Mom's chair, smiling so hard I thought her teeth must hurt. "Delighted you could join us in sunshine land. Isn't the weather fantastic?" She didn't stop for an answer, but instead gave us a five-minute summary of the average number of sunny days per year followed by the annual rainfall statistic. I had never seen anyone before who could talk and smile at the same time, and she was still smiling when she finished.

"Fascinating," Mom said, and I knew she didn't mean it. "You sound as if you're a native."

"Alicia is practically a native," Grandma explained. "She was one of the first—if not *the* first—to buy into the complex." Out of the corner of her mouth, she whispered to me, "Would you believe—three years ago?"

"And you write books, I hear," she continued to Mom.

"Ida doesn't talk much about her family, but I saw you once on one of those morning TV programs."

"Oh—" Mom started to say, but Alicia took control.

"You know, don't you, that Ida is famous, too, around here. She's held the top score in duplicate for the last two months. We think she's unbeatable."

I couldn't remember ever seeing a pack of cards in Grandma's house when she lived on the farm.

"And what are you going to do when you grow up, dear?" She looked past my head and I almost turned around to see if she was talking to someone else standing behind me.

How young did she think I was? Ten? Without thinking, I answered, "Grow older, I suppose—and live in a condo," and realized too late that I was—as Mom always told me—"behaving poorly."

Grandma laughed. Mom cleared her throat. Alicia Halston's smile drooped at one corner, and she stood up smoothing the jogging suit over her nonexistent hips. "Oh, you young people today." She turned to Mom again. "Aren't they a delight?" And she wasn't being sarcastic.

"Tracy," Mother began after the president of the board had walked on. "That was not—"

"That was a perfectly sensible answer, Tracy," Grandma broke in, "to an impossible question. You sounded exactly like your mother."

I wasn't sure whether it was a compliment or not.

"Alicia Halston," Grandma went on, "is boring—boring even when she isn't around."

By lunch, we must have met most of the people who lived in the complex, and all of them seemed to have come from the Midwest. They didn't particularly look that way, but their voices were flat as cornfields.

"We're snowbirds," Grandma said, as if it were some sort of Girl Scout badge. "Displaced persons, really. Did you bring your suit, Tracy? You can spend the afternoon at the pool if you'd like to, or there's a nice little shopping mall within walking distance if you'd rather."

"You're just trying to get rid of me so you can sneak off and take a nap," I kidded.

"Don't be silly. I'm scheduled to play duplicate this afternoon."

"And I have an appointment to meet a friend in town. A psychologist who specializes in adolescents. I thought he might have some suggestions about my next book. Of course, you're welcome to come along, Tracy. . . ." Mom's voice broke off, erasing the welcome from the invitation.

"Don't call them adolescents. It sounds so scraggly and pimply. Besides, I thought you were writing about daughters, not adolescents." I waited for Mom's reaction.

She didn't bother to answer. Instead, she stood up. "I'm going to go in and change."

"Tracy, dear," Grandma said after Mom had left, her voice confidential. "Sometimes you have to be patient with mothers and . . ."

I was sure there was another half to the sentence, but Grandma didn't finish it.

I decided on the shopping mall, after I'd cased the possibility of the pool. A couple of women had taken over the shallow end of the pool and were spending the time alternating between standing and talking and dipping themselves so that the water came just up to their shoulders, never high enough to touch their hair. One man, old enough to be my great-grandfather, swam laps as if he were trying out for the Olympics. I stood there and counted forty, and he was still going when I left. I wondered if Grandma ever used the pool.

I hated shopping malls as much as Amy loved them, but it was Mother's Day weekend and I didn't have a present for either Grandma or Mom. Once shopping for Grandma had been easy—a box of Stover's chocolates, a lavender sachet—but now it was different. As for Mom, she'd pretend to like anything I bought and think I didn't notice.

There were no bargains in the Hacienda Gift Shoppe in Grandma's "nice little mall." A salesperson hovered over my shoulder the minute I came through the door, as if she thought I was going to rip off some of her Gift Shoppe goodies. I circled the Baccarat crystal, bypassed the Lalique and scurried past the Hermes scarves, which left me standing in front of the "Small but Sincere Gifts" counter. The salesperson arched her eyebrows. I pointed. She smiled and pulled out a "small but sincere" box that contained two tiny pink rosebuds of "hand-milled French soap."

"$19.95. Isn't that the loveliest scent you can imagine?"

It was. I bought it.

"Is there anything else?"

There was. A gift for my mother, and the five dollars I had left wasn't enough for "sincere." I finally found a plastic cube filled with notepaper decorated with phony-looking cacti and "Greetings from Arizona" printed on the top sheet. It was the kind of thing a person would put beside a telephone to record important messages, for there was a slot to stick a pen in except the pen was extra so I couldn't buy that. Of course, Mom had an answering machine, but maybe she could use it for grocery lists. Fortunately, gift wrapping wasn't extra.

"Clean hands. Clean heart," Grandma said as she examined her soap. I'm sure she made up the proverb.

"How . . . charming. I can always use notepaper." Mom's words were as small as my gift and just about as sincere.

That last afternoon of our visit, Mom and Grandma kept up a steady stream of do-you-remember's, which can be about as exciting as blow-drying your hair. After a half an hour I felt like an adult watching Mom pretending to be a kid. Instead of slang, the two of them used odd words that they obviously understood but that made no sense to me. At first, Grandma Ida tried to explain. "You see, Tracy," she said, wiping a laugh tear from the corner of her eye, "when your mother was a little girl, she called the blessing that we said before our meals Mini-Min. I think all she was hearing was the amen at the end of the grace and the amen your grandpa always added, which to her meant she could eat. Amen, amen. See? Mini-Min."

The blend of their voices was minus the edge Mom used when she spoke to me. They kept talking about events that didn't exist for me because I hadn't existed, so I sat and listened, eliminated by time until they started talking about Dad. That's when I quit listening and turned on the TV.

On the plane ride home, we had a no-show for seat C, so Mom took the window and I took the aisle. She wanted to talk. I didn't.

"Ida was afraid you weren't having a good time. You did enjoy yourself, didn't you?"

"Yes." It was easy to say yes and not really mean it. Sometimes Mom noticed. Sometimes she didn't.

"She thought you were getting awfully—well, as she said, negative."

I didn't buy that for one minute! Mom was putting her own words in Grandma's mouth. She did that with Dad, too, sometimes, saying he'd asked about something when it was she who wanted to find out.

"When was I negative?" I felt like saying any living, breathing, thinking body couldn't help but be negative sometimes. I didn't. Instead, I started to hum to myself, which I knew drove Mom up the wall, but it often stopped the questions. This time it didn't.

"Does it upset you, Tracy, about your father—his having his own apartment?"

So that was it! Grandma Ida had made her feel guilty, so now what was I supposed to do? At first I thought I'd go ahead and be negative if that's what she and Grandma thought I was; then, because I didn't want to talk about Dad and her, ever, I said, "Doesn't bother me at all. Hardly ever think about it. Why?"

She didn't answer. Instead she turned and looked out the window, even though there was nothing to see but banks of frothy white clouds. "Sometimes I don't understand you, Tracy." She sounded genuinely puzzled.

"There's nothing to understand." I'd used that before, but so many of our nonunderstandings were repeats. "I'm just me. That's all. Take me or leave me. That's the way I happen to be."

"You used to be such an agreeable little girl, but . . . you've changed."

She thought I had changed! How could she be so blind?

Couldn't she see *she* was the one who had changed?

"I've tried to understand, but you don't listen." Mom could be annoyingly reasonable at times, but she was talking to me as if I were a child. When she treated me like a person, we got along. It was when she started telling me what to do, criticizing me, telling me how to do something that the negatives began.

I started to hum again.

She ignored me and went on. "You may listen, but you don't hear."

"I listen," I mumbled. "And I hear."

"Well, I don't *hear* you listening!"

I tried to make sense out of that last remark, but gave up.

For the rest of the trip neither of us talked any more than necessary, but when we did, we had reached the tone-of-voice stage in what I was beginning to think of as our uncivil war. I didn't know how it had started and I didn't know how to stop it, but I was sure it was mostly Mom's fault.

6

THE MINUTE WE ARRIVED HOME, MOM HURried into her study to check on her answering machine. "There's a message for you, Tracy. A Jeff Rogers. He wants you to call him. Do you know him?"

"Sure. He's a senior at Coolidge. Are you sure it was Jeff?"

"If you don't believe me, come listen."

I couldn't imagine why Jeff would phone me. Amy called him a Beautiful Hunk, which he was with the added dimension of a brain. He and I were in Advanced Spanish together one semester, and he had helped me out once on some homework. What could he want with me? The Senior Prom was already over, and he'd be graduating in a few weeks. I thought about talking to Amy first to see if she had any ideas.

I waited until Mom went upstairs to unpack before I flipped on the answering machine, thanking modern technology for recording phone messages when no one was home. I played the message over four times, trying to detect some clue in Jeff's voice that might hint at what he wanted. Finally I gave up and dialed his number. I couldn't believe what I heard! Jeff Rogers—*the* Jeff Rogers—was inviting *me* to his graduation and to his graduation party afterward.

It took barely a minute more before Mom reappeared, carrying her Mother's Day gift as if it were the reason for her coming back downstairs. "Were you able to get in touch with Jeff?"

"You mean what did he want?" I watched her clear off a space for the cube of Arizona notes, search in her desk for a pencil and insert it in the proper slot.

"I did wonder," she admitted.

I took a deep breath and changed voices. After all, I needed her permission, although I'd already told Jeff I'd go. I tried to sound spontaneous. "It's really neat, Mom. Jeff's the guy I told you about. He was in my Spanish class and he's graduating with honors, and he asked me to come see him graduate. You have to have tickets, you know."

"And a party afterward?" I wondered if it were extrasensory perception or the extension phone upstairs.

"He did mention a party afterward," I admitted. The plastic cube of cactus notes looked really chintzy, I noticed, next to the pen-and-pencil set that Dad had given her last Christmas. "It's okay, isn't it?" I said, putting a positive spin on the words. "That I go with Jeff, I mean."

"We'll see," she answered, halfway up the stairs.

Mary Agnes called the "we'll see" answer a universal parental cop-out. I thought it worse than "maybe." It took a week of begging and an appeal to my father, but Mom finally agreed to let me go—with a string of ifs attached.

"If you get home by eleven-thirty."

"I'll be sure to tell Jeff," I promised. "He's very responsible."

"If you're sure Amy and Mary Agnes are going to be there, too."

"They said they had dates."

"And if there's no alcohol."

"Jeff's under age."

From then on, I kept a profile so low that they hardly knew I was around. It wasn't too difficult. Mom was immersed in her research on the adolescent. Dad was busy working on his proposal for saving natural prairies, and school and classes were coasting to a welcome end, punctuated by a couple of brief but definitely appetizing conversations with Jeff. All I needed to do at home was to pretend to be a Mary Agnes and remind myself that up until the last minute Mom could still veto the whole evening.

The night finally arrived. I was in my room making a last-minute decision on whether to wear a white skirt with green sandals or a green skirt with white sandals when I heard a car pull into our drive. I knew Jeff had to be at school early, but this was ridiculous. Then I heard Dad's voice. "Hey. Is the Cricket clad yet?"

Mom answered something that I couldn't hear and Dad laughed. What was he doing here? Mom must have called him. Why were they making such a big production of this? It wasn't as if it were my first date. I'd gone to school dances with Joey Burns and walked home from basketball games with some of the other fellows in my class. Then it was sort of reassuring to have them around, but this was potentially humiliating. Just so Dad didn't start lecturing

Jeff on the preservation of native biomes or worse yet have Mom grill him with loaded questions for her research. There was only one thing to do. Get to the front door first. I chose the white skirt and green sandals and hurried downstairs.

My parents hardly ever sat in the living room. They were usually out in back on the patio, but here they were in their twin La-Z-Boys, one on each side of the fireplace, pretending they weren't living in separate pots.

"Remember the first date we had?" Mom, curled up in her chair like a teenager, was saying.

"Could I forget?" Dad laughed. "Your father took me off in a corner and said—"

"Now take care of my little girl." Mom laughed. "I could have died."

"Then as we were going out the door, your mother said, 'No return on damaged goods.' "

It was like being at Grandma's. They were talking about things that happened before I existed. The doorbell rang, and I walked out of their time warp. "I'll get it," I called back to them, but they were on their feet following me.

Dad reached the door first and opened it, and I think we must have looked like part of a team on "Family Feud." My parents stared at Jeff; Jeff stared at us. I'm not sure who was more surprised: Jeff because we were lined up three abreast or Mom and Dad because Jeff was wearing traditional under-the-graduation-gown garb—ragged cutoffs, Top-Siders, and a T-shirt that read, "Work is a four-letter word."

I was definitely overdressed. I knew I should have worn my green skirt and white sandals. For a minute I thought Mom and Dad were going to whisk me up the stairs and tuck me in for an early bedtime; then I felt both of them take a deep breath and start talking at the same time.

Dad's "You must be Jeff" was laced with Mom's "We're Tracy's parents," probably the two most inane comments I had ever heard my parents utter.

"Great to meet you," Jeff said, shaking Dad's hand and smiling at Mom.

"Have a good time and take care of our little girl," Mom said, obviously grasping for anything to say.

"And no return on . . ." Dad started to say.

I closed my eyes, waiting for the rest of the sentence.

"After eleven-thirty. Right, Jeff?"

"Right, sir. You bet." Jeff shook Dad's hand again.

We headed down the sidewalk toward the car. I glanced back. Mom and Dad stood in the doorway, convulsed in laughter. I didn't see what was so funny.

"Ever been to a graduation?" Jeff backed his newly restored '70 Buick down the drive with one hand on the steering wheel and the other draped nonchalantly across the back of my seat.

"No. Have I missed anything?" I was glad he was asking the questions and not waiting for me to start the conversation.

"It's an old tribal ritual, covered up to look civilized. See. That's my cover-up back there." He pointed to his cap and gown folded neatly on the back seat.

"My parents . . . ," I began, wanting to apologize for their idiotic behavior and not sure how to do it.

"All parents are impossible," Jeff said, as if he really did understand. "But your mom—I saw her on TV. She's a lot cuter in real life. Does she make a lot of money with those books she writes?"

I wondered if Jeff was planning a career as a banker after graduation. "I guess so. She doesn't talk about it." And I didn't want to be talking about my mother, so I tried changing the subject. "The party we're going to afterward. Is it at your house?"

He grinned at me as we turned into the auditorium parking lot. "We'll have to do that one first, but we won't stay long. It'll be cake and ice cream." He parked the car. "I told you parents are impossible. How about meeting you back here after the final rites?" He scooped up his graduation stuff and together we walked toward the other seniors who were milling around the entrance.

The auditorium was filled. The auditorium was hot. The graduation ceremony was long, and I wrote myself a mental note to remember to wear shorts and a tank top next year when I graduated.

The half hour at Jeff's graduation party seemed like three weeks. Not only were his parents there, but all his grandparents, four sets of aunts and uncles, nieces, nephews, and cousins of all ages and sizes, all of whom I had to meet.

"This is Jeff's friend, Tracy. She's Welda Spencer's daughter. You know, the one who writes books. She was on TV a few weeks ago."

By the time I'd met everyone, I wondered if his parents had insisted Jeff invite me as an added attraction. One good thing, though—everyone was so impressed with my mother's name that there were no funny comments about mine. Just as I was refusing a third slice of sheet cake, Jeff muttered, "Let's split." I almost beat him to the car, happy to leave the ghost of Welda Spencer's daughter circulating among the relatives.

The next three parties were almost indistinguishable from each other except for the music, the beer, and the number of empty cans that had accumulated during the evening. Kids, who at school were brains, jocks, preppies, or "good kids," now seemed intent on seeing how bombed they could get and how fast they could get there. It was like watching a relay race with beer cans instead of batons.

I stuck with a diet Coke and Jeff had only half a beer at each place, mainly because we didn't stay long enough for him to drink a whole one.

"Now for the real party," Jeff said, grabbing my arm.

"You mean those weren't real?" We could still hear the heavy-metal beat as we drove away.

"No. This next one's the grand finale. We've been planning it all semester."

We were headed down a residential street, Jeff concentrating on his driving as if we were being tailed by a cop. Expanses of lawns led up to sprawling ranch houses with attached garages and the sedate northern colonial two-stories with fake shutters. It was what realtors called a "good neighborhood." No beer blasts here.

"We aren't going to Zumwalt Station, are we?" Once had been more than enough for me.

He took his eyes off the street for a minute and smiled approvingly. "Hey. You're more of a party girl than I thought. No wonder you haven't had anything to drink. You been saving up for the good stuff, right?" He checked the speedometer and slowed the car. "Not Zumwalt. That's what the cops will be expecting. *You can get . . . anything you want . . . at Spurlock's Gravel Pits,*" he sang to the tune of Arlo Guthrie's old song, "Alice's Restaurant."

He had me wrong! I was no party girl. What I had meant was "Oh, please not Zumwalt Station." I sneaked a look at my wristwatch. It was ten-thirty already.

"I have to be home in an hour. Do we have time?"

"Don't worry. We won't stay long."

We drove off on a side street that, after several miles, turned into a gravel road and then after more miles branched off into a dirt road that wound along beside a creek. I remembered tramping around down along this creek with Dad, looking for what someone had reported was an orange wood lily. He didn't find one.

Tree branches slapped across our windshield as our headlights barely lit up the road ahead, until a sharp turn revealed—not the Pits but more road. I did begin to worry. At this rate it would take until eleven-thirty to find our way back out of the Pits.

We began to hear music. Mom says whenever I get nervous, I chatter. "Isn't it funny," I said, peering off into the distance trying to locate where the music was coming from, "how the bass notes are always the ones you hear first and vice versa. The ones that fade last?"

Jeff laughed as if it really *were* funny and reached over to squeeze my knee. "Hey, Trace. You're a riot. We should have done this a long time ago."

I wasn't so sure, as we pulled up beside a long line of parked cars.

"Come on." Jeff grabbed my hand. "Here's where the fun begins."

Somebody had started a bonfire, and in the flickering of the flames kids were dancing to yet another heavy-metal group. A pickup was parked close by, and on its open tailgate stood a row of beer kegs that were doing a heavy business. I supposed that was where Jeff would head, but he pulled me toward a station wagon on the other side of the truck.

"I'm a beer man, myself," he shouted in my ear, "but graduation calls for something stronger." He let go of my arm long enough to trade fake punches with a couple of his buddies and grab two plastic cups that I knew were not filled with Kool-Aid. "Drink up," he said more quietly, as the music subsided. "I can drive home with my eyes shut."

I took the cup he handed me and looked out over the crowd of kids, thinking that except for the fact that what we were doing was totally illegal, this could have been a high school homecoming pep rally. By the time I turned back to Jeff, he'd finished drinking whatever was in his cup to the shouts of the other guys chanting, "Chug it! Chug it!" I was feeling like a lost kid in a supermarket when someone poked me in the back.

"In case you haven't figured it out, this really *is* the pits. Small *p.*" Amy wafted up beside me, minus her date. "Come on." She waved at Jeff. "We'll be back in a minute." He waved to us in return, spilling part of the contents of his refilled cup.

The music started again and drowned out any chance of our talking until we reached a path that led down toward the water. No one was sure how deep the Pits really were, although I'd heard Dad say he thought around forty to fifty feet, since most of the roads in the county were surfaced with the gravel.

"What time are you supposed to be home?" I sat down on an upended boulder. Amy stretched out on the grass beside me.

"Eleven-thirty, of course. Is there ever life after eleven-thirty?"

"Where's Brent?"

"About two ahead of Jeff. The last time I saw him, he was pretending he was Peter Pan."

"Want some?" I offered her my untouched cup.

"I've tried it, and my candied opinion is—don't. I'm not sure what they're pouring, but I think it's lethal. It tastes like cough medicine."

I took a small sip and poured what was left on the ground.

"How you getting home? With Brent?"

"Not me." She crumpled her plastic cup. "Guess who's here."

"Grunt? I mean, Boyd?"

"Are you kidding? Mary Agnes . . . with Stanley."

"Together? You mean they crashed the party? I thought it was just for seniors and their dates, and I thought Mary Agnes told me she had a date."

"She did—with Stanley, and you know Mary Agnes. She never has to crash anything; she just materializes and nobody seems to mind. And Stanley? Well, you know Stanley."

"Sometimes I wish I didn't." I picked up a stone and tossed it toward the water where it hit, making a small gulping sound. "He's changed."

"Not really. Our boy genius is just discovering the social scene. He's just a late bloomer, is all."

The gravel crunched behind us. We turned as Mary Agnes and Stanley emerged from the darkness, slipping and sliding on the loose rocks.

"Shall we have a meeting of *next* year's senior class?" she called. "Anyway, it was time to detach Stanley from the keg before his face turned to foam."

Stanley looked nothing like the zombie we'd hauled to that lonely tent after the Zumwalt Station disaster. Maybe he'd learned how to handle the party routine. The only thing that bothered me was that he couldn't seem to stop grinning and nobody had said anything funny.

"So what do you think?" he asked. "Is this a lousy excuse for a party or what? Here it is a perfect night for swimming, but nobody will go with me."

"Sit down and take a few deep breaths of oxygen," Amy said. "Can't you see most of the guys are too drunk and most girls don't wear bathing suits to graduation? So what else is new besides the fact that you haven't fallen on your face yet?"

"Give him another ten minutes or another beer. Whichever comes first. Stanley isn't just a cheap drunk; he's a blue-light, K Mart special." Mary Agnes patted his head.

"Stanley," I said, "when did you start being a lush?"

"Get out of my face," he muttered, still grinning at nothing. "What's with you? Since when did you guys get so pure?"

"We've always been nice girls." Amy cupped her chin with both thumbs, tilted her head and smiled sweetly.

"In the interest of your possible future, Stanley, why don't you let me take you home? And you too." Mary Agnes turned to Amy and me. "You'd better come with us because Brent is asleep in the back of Jeff's car, and the last I saw, Jeff had lost his car keys and was crawling on his hands and knees looking for them."

"No way!" Stanley shook his head. "I'm doing research

for *our* party next year. I'm going to make a list—"

"If you stay here, the only listing you'll be doing is to starboard—or maybe I mean port." Amy wasn't laughing. "The next thing, you'll be mixing beer with the hard stuff, and that's deadly."

"Hard stuff!" He sounded offended. "I don't do that. Think I'm crazy? I did smoke pot once. . . ." He was quiet for a minute. "And I've had just one beer tonight, I think."

"You're getting to be a bad habit." Mary Agnes's voice was oddly adult. "This could be the second time we've rescued you."

He laughed. "Yeah, but I don't remember the first time, so that didn't count. I didn't even put it down in The Book."

"How can you be so dumb?" I asked.

"I like the way I feel. It's just that simple, and it's not dumb."

None of us had an answer.

"Besides," he went on, "being high is better than dying of boredom."

The three of us looked at each other in silence until Amy said, "Trace, I don't know about you, but I am going to be killed if I don't get home on time."

"Want to start walking?" I asked.

Mary Agnes jingled her keys and turned to go. "I'd look upon this as an act of mercy if you'd come with us, Stanley."

Without waiting for us, he started scrambling back up the bank. "Don't sweat it. I have everything under control." He began to run. "The guys will take me home," he called back.

We made it to Amy's house at twenty to twelve and to mine three minutes later. It wasn't perfect, but it was a near miss so I didn't expect any hassle from Mom.

I stuck my head back in the car before Mary Agnes drove away. "Thanks a lot," I said. "You're a saint."

"Not yet," she answered, "but it's good for my self-image."

As I shut the front door of our house behind me and double-checked the lock, Mom and Dad emerged from the kitchen.

"Tracy," Mom began. "Have you seen Stanley tonight?"

"Why?" I leaned against the front door and hoped they hadn't noticed that it wasn't Jeff who'd brought me home. "Is something wrong?"

I wasn't too surprised that Mom was still up. She always checked me in like some kind of time clock, but Dad should have been in his apartment across town.

"Nothing, we hope," Dad said, "but Bob called. Stanley isn't home yet. He told his folks he was going to a graduation party and he'd be home around ten. And you know how precise Stanley is."

At that very moment, Stanley was probably precisely drunk or stoned or both, but I wasn't about to rat on him. I couldn't tell them everything I knew without getting involved in a no-win discussion of how I'd spent the evening.

"Was he at Jeff's party?" Mom was a stickler for details.

"No," I answered, glad I could tell the truth.

She turned to Dad. "Oh, you know how Mavis and Bob worry. I don't believe they realize what a responsible young man he is. Has been since he was small."

I hoped he was responsible enough not to have staggered into one of the pits. I could still hear the small gulping sound the stone had made when I tossed it into the water. Certainly Jeff or Brent or someone would take care of him, try to sober him up and bring him home.

"Well," Dad said, as if to dismiss Stanley from further consideration, "we haven't asked you, Cricket, if you had a good time. Jeff seems like a fine young man."

"I met his family." I started for the stairs. "All of them, and they asked me a lot of questions about you, Mom, and your books." I was pretty sure that would put an end to any more questions, so I started on up the stairs with a "I'm tired. I'm going to bed. Good night."

"Say, Cricket, don't forget next weekend," Dad called after me. "The camp-out."

"I won't."

"And next time you see Stanley, tell him we'll need his tent."

7

I MADE IT A POINT TO SEE STANLEY, AND IT wasn't Dad's casual "next time," either. I wanted my money back that he'd borrowed. La Petite Miss was having a presummer sale on bathing suits, and Mary Agnes and Amy and I were going to go shopping that next Wednesday afternoon since it was final-exam week at school and our only test was in the morning.

I hadn't seen Stanley since the Pits party, but, after searching all over school one afternoon the next week, I caught him down by the boys' locker room.

"What are you doing down here?"

He was sitting by himself on a bench.

"Helping Coach check in equipment." He closed his notebook and started to leave.

I knew that wasn't really what he was doing, but I didn't care whether he was checking in or checking out, just so he wasn't planning to check out on me. "I thought you were going to pay back the money you borrowed. You said you'd have it for me Monday."

"I missed school Monday." He sort of grinned. "I didn't feel so good."

"Hung over, you mean."

"Okay. Hung over."

"Your folks called looking for you." I followed him across the gym and out the side door.

"They found me. On the front lawn. The fellas dumped me off."

"How dumb can you get, Stanley! What did your folks say?"

"No big deal. I told them I had a touch of food poisoning from something I'd eaten. They were going to rush me to the hospital, but I talked them out of it."

"They believed you?"

"Apparently."

We cut across the football practice field, through Crocker Elementary's playground, and down Whitfield's Alley. It was our own special way of going home when we were in grade school, to avoid the big kids. We always used to walk home together then, but for some reason that stopped when we reached junior high.

"Anyway"—he really grinned now—"I got my driver's license last week. A bunch of us are going swimming down at the Pits. You and Amy and Mary Agnes want to come along?"

"Can't. Have to finish that term paper for history."

"The old man's going to let me have the car. He's finally decided little Stanley's grown up."

"If you're going to be driving a car," I began as we turned up my street, "you can't go on getting stoned out of your cotton-picking mind. You're going to be a confirmed alcoholic before we graduate."

"What are you talking about?" He walked on ahead. "It takes years to become an alcoholic."

"But you get so bombed. What's wrong? You trying to prove something? Trying to be Big Man on Campus at Coolidge?"

"Of course not," he growled. "And who are you to preach? You and Mary Agnes and Amy tip a few whenever you get a chance."

"We don't get sloppy drunk!"

"So what?"

I grabbed his arm to make him stop walking a step ahead of me and lowered my voice. "One beer and you're out of your gourd. At least, that's what Boyd told me."

He jerked his arm loose. "Since when do you believe what Boyd says? Anyway, I told you. I like the way it makes me feel. Happy. Relaxed. Glowing."

We stopped in front of my house. Usually I ran up the walk with a "See ya," but this time I didn't want him to leave.

"I worry about you, Stanley." It was the nicest thing I'd ever said to him.

He looked at me, half puzzled.

"Don't!" he said, brushing his hand against my cheek.

I felt as if I was going to cry. He turned and walked on up the street.

"Hey!" I called after him. "Where's my forty dollars?"

"I'll get it for you this weekend. Okay?"

It was not okay, but it was Stanley. What else could I do? So I'd have to con Mom out of her charge card if I was going shopping the next day for a bathing suit.

From long experience, I knew exactly how to con Mom: do something useful around the house without being told.

I ticked off things that might soften her up. I could clean out the hall closet or wash her car or vacuum and dust the den and living room. The hall closet held mostly Dad's things, so that was out. The weather forecast was promising rain the next day, besides Mom's car was never really dirty, and the house didn't look bad enough for all that vacuuming and dusting.

The laundry. Of all the things Mom had to do, she hated doing the laundry worst of all. She'd toss the dirty clothes in and start the washer going and then get interested in her writing and maybe six or seven hours later she'd remember she hadn't transferred the wet clothes into the dryer. The same with the dryer. She'd forget to take clothes out when they were dry and when she did they were all permanently creased into wrinkles.

When I got home, the door to Mom's study was ajar, and I could hear the hum of her word processor.

"Tracy?" she called. "There are some chocolate-chip cookies on the kitchen counter. I felt like baking this morning."

No wonder I weighed more than Mom did. As long as I could remember, there had always been some kind of snack waiting in the kitchen when I came home from school. Mom didn't look at food so much as a source of nourishment as she did as a reward for good behavior or a peace offering after an argument or the "I love you" that she seldom said aloud.

"Later," I called back. "I've got some stuff to do first."

I started with my own room. In the process of getting the sheets off, I made the mistake of looking under my bed, where I found two pairs of shorts and a tank top that I'd been looking for the last two weeks. I stuffed all the clothes from the laundry hamper, plus the odds and ends from the bottom of my closet, into a bundle with the sheets and dragged it all into the hallway.

Before attacking Mom's bedroom, I sat down on the top step to rest. Mom's word processor droned on. If she'd just listen to me, I could give her a whole chapter of dialogue between mothers and daughters. In the first place, the mother would be appreciative of whatever the daughter was trying to do, like, "How can I thank you enough? How thoughtful of you to take care of a job that I loathe, and you've done it just when I needed it most." "Now, Mother," I'd say, "sometimes we don't get along, but I'm trying hard to understand. You've changed in the last couple of years. You're so bossy, always telling me what to do, and I can't see why you don't trust me. . . ."

My pretend conversation was cut short with Mom shouting from downstairs, "I forgot to tell you. Your dad called to tell you to pack your poncho. There's rain forecast for the weekend."

It didn't take long to pick up in Mom's room. She was incredibly neat. Even the soiled clothes were folded and stacked. Her bed wasn't even rumpled, but I stripped it anyway and felt like a Girl Scout working for a merit badge. I was headed downstairs, with enough laundry to ground a camel—I'd forgotten the upstairs bathroom—when it occurred to me that if I was really going to do the dutiful daughter routine, I'd have to remake both beds. I almost quit right there and then. Here I was doing this drudgery to be kind—well, sort of kind—but if I were a mother it would be part of my job description. I vowed again I would think twice before *I* ever became a mother.

Mom stuck her head into the laundry room just as I was

finishing up on the last load of things in the dryer. She looked a little as if she'd been on gentle spin herself.

"I think I've got it, Tracy! The first line for the first chapter." She leaned against the empty washing machine and read from a typed sheet: "Orthoepically, *daughter* and *laughter* are analogous, differing only in their initial letters of *d* and *l.* In real-life situations, however, having the former demands the latter."

"There's an awful lot of big words, don't you think?" I said as I folded the last of what seemed like enough towels to supply the Calvin Coolidge football team for an entire semester.

I didn't think she heard me, for she was busy *refolding* the stack of towels into her own idea of perfection. I decided the use of her charge card wasn't worth the effort.

I didn't need the credit card anyway, because we didn't go shopping. We went to visit Stanley—in the hospital!

"Did you hear about Stanley?" Mary Agnes came sprinting down the hall that next morning with Amy lagging behind.

"No! What's wrong?" I grabbed my pen and notebook from my locker and ran to join them.

"Wrecked his dad's car last night." Amy rolled her eyes.

"Is he all right?" Stanley was invincible. Nothing terrible could happen to Stanley.

"We think so. They're keeping him in the hospital a couple of days for observation. Hurry through this stupid test and we'll go see him."

The hospital wasn't *observing* Stanley very carefully because when we located his room, he wasn't even in bed.

He was standing looking out the window, his back to us.

"Don't jump, Stanley dear. We're here!" Mary Agnes shouted from the doorway. "All's right with the world."

He half turned. "Wasn't going to jump, Mary Agnes. I was counting the parking spaces down there. Do you know how many cars they can accommodate at one time? Would you believe 120 plus 16 compacts?"

It was the old Stanley, and I wanted to hug him, but I didn't think he'd understand.

"What happened?" I think he knew I would be the one to ask that.

He turned back to the window. "Well, it's a long, short story. I think what happened . . ." He paused and turned around. He had a patch across his forehead and down across his nose.

"What do you mean *think?*" Mary Agnes was being Miss Pure.

"I'm not sure. I really can't remember much. All I know is I had the accelerator almost floored. I suppose we were going about seventy down the interstate when one of the guys hollered, 'Shift her into overdrive.' And I did. Only I hit reverse. We came to a grinding stop. Automatic transmissions are dangerous."

"How'd you get home?" Amy sat down in the one available chair.

"Left the car on the shoulder and walked until we found a phone and called home. I guess I stripped the gears; at least old Dad is going to trade it in. So my driving career has come to a grinding stop, too. I guess Mom and Dad are disappointed in me."

I didn't ask any more.

"Stanley, dear." Mary Agnes took over in her mother-mentor tone. "You will *have* to learn how to drink before you drive."

Amy laughed.

"But I only had one beer." From where I stood, it looked as if his nose were broken.

"Maybe you should switch to rum," Amy suggested with a wink at me.

I didn't wink back. What all year had been just a fun escape from prying parents—sneaking a little rum now and then and an occasional beer blast—was turning into something else.

"What did the windshield look like?" Amy went on.

"All I remember is seeing stars." Stanley sat down on the edge of the bed. "No one else got hurt, though. Dad had the car towed in. Didn't even have to make an accident report, but he insisted on bringing me here to the hospital."

"Would you like us to bring you flowers?" Amy looked around the bare room.

"Depends on what kind of flowers." Stanley grinned, then winced as he touched the bandages on his face.

"You look like a raccoon. But, Stanley-boy," Mary Agnes assumed her school counselor voice. "There's no rush about it all. You have a whole lifetime to live it up."

"More like an albino raccoon," Amy added.

"What if I prefer to live it up today?" He did look like an albino raccoon.

"Then you'll have no tomorrow, Sledge Head," Mary Agnes snapped back in her own nastiest voice.

"I happen to prefer to detach myself from the past as well as the future, both of which exist only in the imagination." Stanley was being his usual obnoxious self, talking in complete abstractions that never made any sense to me or any difference either, for that matter.

"Oh, the heroic egotism of genius!" Mary Agnes moaned, holding her head in mock agony. "But remember, my dear boy, the present is the prelude to the future."

"Where'd you read that?"

"In the yellow pages," Mary Agnes smirked. Mary Agnes loved nothing better than trying to argue Stanley down—all in fun, of course—but I had a feeling this was not all for fun.

"I thought so," Stanley countered. "Anyway, who wants to live in the contaminated future that we're facing?"

For a second, I almost wished Mom were with me. If she thought she wanted to write a book about adolescents—and daughters in particular—she should be listening to what Stanley and Mary Agnes were saying rather than researching in libraries or talking to a psychologist in Arizona.

We finally said good-bye to Stanley, trooped noisily down the hospital corridor, piled into Mary Agnes's car, drove down to the Pits and did a three-way split on a warm beer Mary Agnes had stashed under her driver's seat.

BY THE TIME SCHOOL WAS OUT FOR THE SUMmer, I was still waiting for my forty dollars from Stanley, but I'd stopped hounding him for it. After all, in a way he'd done me a favor. Mom was so caught up in the details of his accident that she'd forgotten to quiz me further on my graduation fiasco with Jeff.

In fact, I thought I was home free until Mom came roaring out of her study with, "Young lady . . ."

When mothers start out with "young lady," it is not intended as a badge of achievement.

"What's this call on my answering machine from Jeff? He says he's sorry about graduation night and did you have any trouble getting home?"

"I haven't the slightest," I answered, stalling for time to think. One of my best defenses, however, had always been to counter a question with another question. "When did he call?"

"I am not interested in *when* he called. I am interested in *why* he called."

"I am, too," I agreed. "I'll go call him. Do you want

to get on the extension and listen?" I knew that would make her mad, but I was fighting to save my image. If she ever found out about the beer bust, she'd ground me for the rest of the summer. I should have known better, though, than to resort to sarcasm with Mom. She could out-sarcast me any day.

"Now, Tracy." She lowered her voice threateningly. "Don't be that way."

"There you go again, Mother." I grabbed at the chance to steer her away from more questions. "What do you mean '*that* way'? It happens to be the way I am, and I'm sorry I can't do everything your way, because it so happens I'm not you."

"I don't expect you to be. And that is not the question. But I do expect you to answer a question honestly and straightforwardly when I ask it."

"So?" I fired back. "What's the question?"

I really didn't like what we were doing. I didn't like the way we were sounding. I didn't like the way Mom's face was drawn up tight, her eyes little slits and her mouth a thin, lipless line, but once we started, we couldn't seem to stop.

Mom turned away, took a deep breath and lowered her voice to an unbearably patient level. "I am merely asking you, if Jeff didn't bring you home, who did and why?"

It wasn't "merely one" question. It was *two,* but Mom could never argue fair.

"Mary Agnes brought me home. Jeff couldn't find his car keys." I knew I shouldn't have mentioned that last part.

Mom wasted no time in jumping in with, "You mean no one at Jeff's house had a spare set?"

I'd answered my way into a dead end. There was no other way but the truth—or part of it, at least. "It was a different party." I looked her straight in the eye. I could stare down Dad that way. It never worked with Mom.

"And where was this party?" Why did she have to sound so triumphant?

I tried to weasel out of answering that one. With Mom, one answer led to at least a dozen more questions. "Oh, Mom! Can't we discuss all this later? Dad'll be here any minute for the camp-out, and I still haven't got all my stuff together."

"He won't be here for another half hour." She settled herself on the couch. "Where did you say this other party was?"

"I didn't."

"It wasn't out at Spurlock's Gravel Pits, was it?"

Sometimes I was amazed how much mothers knew. On the other hand, we were neatly past the other three beer parties we'd been to, so she had missed a few details.

"We just drove by to see what was going on," I said, trying not to sound defensive. "We were on our way home. I was only about ten minutes late." I was glad she couldn't know how fast Mary Agnes had driven. "Besides, all the other kids were there."

She sat up straighter and leaned toward me. "Tracy, if all the other kids decided to jump in the water and drown, would you have done it, too?"

It was a rotten question, and there was no way I could answer it. "Look. It was no big deal. Okay?"

"No! It is not okay! You didn't tell your father and me anything about going to the Pits." She didn't look angry anymore. She looked kind of old and tired.

"You didn't ask me. I didn't lie about anything." I crossed my fingers and exed out Stanley. "All you asked was did I have a good time at Jeff's party."

Mom stood up. "Tracy Spencer, you are acting like a ten-year-old. Withholding part of the truth is a form of lying."

"People do it all the time. Important people, I mean."

"What was going on at the Pits? And what was the matter with Jeff that he couldn't bring you home?"

There was no use. She had me cornered. I gave up. "Jeff was drunk."

Mom sat back down. She was even pretty when she was angry.

"So," I went on, "like I said, Mary Agnes brought us home. Amy and me. Brent was drunk, too." I kept thinking the more times I mentioned Mary Agnes's name the better chance I had of getting myself out of the mess. It didn't work.

"And you didn't think it necessary to tell your father and me about this?"

"Not really. I got home all right. I thought you'd just be upset if . . ."

"I am upset!" Her words came out in angry little bites. She stood up again and started for her study.

"Mary Agnes and Amy and I weren't drinking!" I shouted after her. "And if you don't believe me, ask them."

She acted as if she didn't hear me. "You may go with your father this weekend, but when you get back, consider yourself grounded until you can start acting like a responsible human being."

I opened my mouth to object. I had been responsible,

I thought, but I knew when I'd been outmaneuvered. Why couldn't she let me live my own life? She'd always told me to think for myself, and then when I did, she didn't like it. Talk about inconsistent! When I was little, she always told me to "be a big girl. Stand on your own feet." Now that I *was* a "big girl" she cut my legs out from under me.

I stomped up the stairs to finish packing for the weekend, but Mom, who always insisted on having the last word, called, "I don't care what you think about me right now, Tracy, but don't you *dare* say it out loud!"

I was so ticked that I didn't even bother to answer when she called, "Have a good time," as I went out the door. I threw my backpack down and sat on the front steps to wait for Dad, although I knew he wouldn't be coming for another fifteen minutes. Maybe I could convince him to let me stay with him for a week or so. At least I'd be out of the house and away from Mom.

When Dad said, "Hi, Tracy," instead of calling me Cricket, as I climbed into the van, I knew Mom must have phoned to tell him about my brief life as a party girl, and I prepared for a second lecture. Instead, as we pulled away from the house, he said, "Hope you're ready for some real work. We'll set up camp tonight and get started as soon as the sun's up tomorrow."

"I thought Stanley was coming." I checked out the back of the van to make sure he wasn't lurking behind the pile of tents, sleeping bags, and air mattresses.

"He and his dad left about an hour ago with the others. They should all be there by now. Did you remember your rain gear? It may be wet tomorrow."

Of course, I hadn't remembered. I'd been so busy fighting with Mom that the message slipped my mind. "What others?" I asked. "I thought it was going to be just the four of us."

"Chris. You remember. You met her the night we had dinner. And two of our graduate students. We could use a couple more people, but this is strictly volunteer labor. It should be fun, though."

Since one of Dad's ideas of fun consisted of stuff like counting how many seeds came from one milkweed pod, I didn't get my hopes up. At least I wasn't stuck home, grounded with Mom, where I was likely to be for the rest of the summer until I figured out her exact definition of "responsible."

Setting up my tent wasn't exactly hilarious either since it collapsed on me twice just when I thought I had it subdued. "I think it's alive," I told Stanley when he finally ambled over to help.

"Did you try reading the instructions? I think you skipped a step, like maybe the first one." This was basic Stanley, and I had trouble matching him with the larger-than-life party boy he was becoming.

"Of course I didn't look at the instructions. I'm too creative for that." By the time I had the sentence out of my mouth, he had the tent set up, looking sturdy enough to last until the next ice age.

We stood around talking about what we'd be doing for the rest of the summer. Stanley was looking for a job—*he* said. Maybe I'd get my forty dollars back after all. I had no intention of being gainfully employed, but I began to wonder if I could escape Mom's grounding if I found a job.

"Hey, son," Stanley's father called. "We need that biota count list and I can't find it."

"Be right there." He turned to go. "That's all I need—

his prowling through my backpack. I think my folks are paranoid. You know how it is." He loped off without waiting for an answer, but he was right. I *did* know how it was.

By noon of the next day, I was schizophrenic. Dad hadn't been kidding when he said we were going to start at daybreak; in fact, as far as I was concerned, the sliver of moon was brighter than the faint pink of a sun that hadn't even risen. By the time I had gulped down some milk and half a sweet roll, Dad and Chris had everybody organized and had given me so many errands to run that I felt as if I were ready for the high school relay team.

Afternoon wasn't much better, but it was different. Dad, Bob Prentice, and Stanley still plodded around with survey equipment trying to figure out boundary lines. Chris commandeered me and the two graduate students, who acted as if they were on a quest for the Grail or something. She'd marked off a series of little areas with stakes and strings, and we were supposed to count how many different kinds of plants were growing in the squares.

It seemed easy enough at first, especially when I found out that I didn't actually have to know what the plants *were;* I only had to count and record them. That was lucky because I could barely tell a dandelion from a milkweed. But after the first fifteen minutes, I'd lost track of what I'd counted and had to begin again. "Back to square one," I said as Chris came over to check on my progress. In spite of having spent most of the day upended in prairie grass and hundreds of little sticky, weedlike flowers, she looked remarkably unfrazzled. I wondered if that were some kind of magic that came with adulthood. Even the graduate students looked less seedy than Stanley or I.

She peered at my little plot, which was kind of squashed because at first I'd thought it was possible to sit down and count at the same time. "Little bluestem and side oats grama," she murmured, as if it were some kind of incantation. "Do you begin to sense the wonder of this place, Tracy? This vegetation has been here for eons."

I'd never been too sure just how long an eon was and the only kind of wonder I felt was about how I'd gotten myself into this, but I grinned and nodded. "Biomes *are* beautiful, aren't they?" I didn't want to spoil her enthusiasm, and I did like her—sort of. She knew how to get people to do things without ordering them around.

"I've always thought so. That's why it's so terrific to be working on this project with your father." She hunkered down beside me and patted a little fungus-looking plant that I'd been trying to stay clear of. "Are you interested in science or are you going to be an artist like your mother?"

Mom would have loved the sound of that word—artist. "She's not an artist, though." I made an X for the fungus. "She writes books."

"Oh, but writing is an art. At least writing as well as she does is." She picked up a fuzzy black and orange caterpillar and let it crawl across her palm. "I've read her books and I think she's terrific. The only things I can write are academic articles."

She sounded as sincere about Mom's writing as she had about eons, so I smiled as if I agreed and said, "Dad told me he's really glad you came here—to the university, I mean. Most of the people in his department aren't really interested in prairie grass and stuff." He hadn't told me that, but I thought it sounded like something he might have said.

"I'm glad, too. But I'd better get back to work." She stood up. "You're doing great, Tracy. Just a few more plots and we'll take a break. I've a cooler of Cokes. How's that for incentive?"

I hunched over my last corner of green stuff and continued the count. The incentive turned out to be a mirage, because work went on without a break until almost sunset. By that time, I knew I'd developed a permanent stoop. I also knew that my counting would probably ruin the reliability of their figures—after the first hour, all those green plants had looked remarkably the same.

When Dad and the others got back, we finally sprawled out in front of the tents and listened while he launched into an enthusiastic account of what they'd discovered. After a few minutes, I tuned out his words and just listened to the excitement in his voice. I'd never understood how people could care so much about the idea of something. With Dad it was prairie preservation, with Mom it was writing. As for me, the only thing I really wanted was to be out of high school and as far away from home as possible.

Watching Dad and Chris, together, trying to explain some obscure point about prairie ecosystems, I wondered, for just a minute, what it would be like if they were my parents. They couldn't be, of course; I already had a mother and I was almost positive that Dad wouldn't ever mess around. Not that I'd blame him. After Mom's unfairness the afternoon before, I thought that maybe it was her fault that Dad had moved out. He could do that because he was an adult. I was trapped.

"Hi, Trace." Stanley sat down beside me. He was still wearing a white patch across his forehead and down over his nose. He really did look like an inquisitive raccoon as he flipped through the pages on his clipboard and then tossed it aside. "I'm getting bored with botany, aren't you?"

"Yeah. But what else is there to do in a prairie patch?"

"Let's take a walk."

I glanced at Dad, but he didn't look up. "Sure. Why not?"

"We're going to check out the bat population," Stanley called to his father as we headed up the hill behind our tents. His father didn't pay any attention, either.

We hadn't taken more than a few dozen steps before Stanley said, "You couldn't lend me a ten, could you? Maybe."

I stopped. "Stanley!" I almost screamed. "You haven't paid me my forty dollars yet!"

"I know. I know." He glanced back over his shoulder as if he thought someone might have heard me. "Give me a little time. I'll get your money for you."

"What do you need ten dollars for?" This time I was going to know where my money was going. Always, before, Stanley was the one who had the cash on hand, and if any of us ran short before allowance day, it was Stanley who would see us through.

"Have to take the SAT over."

"What do you mean over? You didn't take it in the first place."

"I started to." He laughed. "But I didn't feel like doing it that day, so I walked out. Told them I was sick. Now

I have to reregister. Dad gave me the money, but I spent it. All I need is ten. I got part of it."

"Where?" I knew without asking.

"From Mary Agnes."

"And Amy?"

"And Amy."

It took us only about ten minutes to climb the small hill behind our camp; in fact, it was the only hill around. Except for the few acres of undisturbed prairie we'd left, flat cropland, fields with faint green rows of corn or soybeans, spread to the horizon, dotted here and there with silos and farmsteads.

"This is far enough," Stanley said, slouching down at the base of a tall cottonwood tree that crowned the rise.

"Far enough for what?"

An evening star glimmered even though the sky was still streaked with sunset. For once Dad had been wrong in his weather prediction.

"Happy time." He pulled a joint from his shirt pocket. "I've some more in my backpack, but I figured maybe we could share one."

It wasn't the fact that he had a joint that surprised me. It was how casually he offered it, as if the two of us were merely going to split a Hershey bar or something.

"No, thanks," I blurted out, trying to sound as if I were accustomed to turning down pot every day. "Aren't you afraid you'll get caught? I mean, with your dad down there?"

"What about my dad?" He attached the wilted cigarette to a funny metal holder, and cupping the end in one hand, lit it.

"Won't he smell you?"

"One little joint in the open air? Never." He took a puff, holding the smoke inside as he leaned back up against the tree.

"But your dad will notice if you get high."

He blew the smoke out lazily. The fumes drifted over to me. "He'll never notice. He only notices what he hopes to see."

"How can you be so lucky? My mom notices everything I do, and I do mean everything." I really hadn't looked closely before, but Stanley was growing a little fuzz on his upper lip; in fact, it wouldn't have hurt him to start shaving. "You know, don't you, that you shouldn't be fooling around with this crazy stuff. They've told us about it since fifth grade, or weren't you listening?"

"I listened. I even took notes, but they didn't tell us a little pot makes everything fit. All the things you think are wrong get to be so funny you can't stop laughing."

A meadowlark called from some distant field, a sad and lonesome call that seemed to hang in the still air.

"Don't worry, Tracy. I'm in control. I can stop any time I want."

"Sure. Sure." I sounded like Mom. "You can handle it. I've seen you wasted out of your mind. You're going to fry your brains someday."

"How about you and Amy and Mary Agnes? What makes you think the three weird sisters are immune? That's not water you pour in your Cokes, is it?"

"That's different," I said. "We do it for fun and *we* do know when to stop. Besides, we don't do it *every* weekend. And," I added triumphantly, "we don't do drugs."

"Pot's not really a drug. Not like coke or crack. I

wouldn't mess with that stuff. Anyway, you're not going to rat on me, are you?"

"When did I ever rat on you, Stanley?"

"I'll have to look in The Book." He started giggling as if he'd said something really funny. "Don't sweat it. I'm just seeing what it's like. And for once, I'm doing something I want to do, not what my father expects. You know what I mean?"

I knew, but the evening was much darker now and I thought we should start back. "Shouldn't we go? What if someone comes out looking for us?"

"It'd blow my cover, wouldn't it?" He sat up, took another long drag and carefully pinched off the burning end of the cigarette.

"You save the butt?"

"Of course. This stuff's expensive."

"Where do you get it?" Not that I really wanted to know or expected Stanley to tell me.

"Anyplace. You ask someone to get it for you who knows someone who knows someone else. It's easy." He stood up and started down the hill.

I wanted to ask him if that was how he'd spent my forty dollars—on pot—but I didn't because that would have made me something I didn't want to be.

I hurried after him. "How do you know you won't get hooked?"

"I told you I can handle it. Besides, I like how it makes me feel. And maybe I don't want to be straight."

I couldn't get anywhere arguing with him. We walked along without saying anything until he stopped and stared down at the ground. "That's funny. It feels like the grass is growing clear up around my ankles."

We weren't walking in grass! We were walking down the middle of a gravel road.

"It wasn't too bad, was it?" Dad said the next morning as I threw my gear into the back of the van. I'd held a surveyor's rod for Stanley's dad until I felt like a flagpole myself. I'd carried one end of a measuring tape for Dad, wading ankle-deep among puffs of what Dad called Grandfather's Whiskers but Chris maintained was Prairie Smoke, and I'd been the designated run-and-getter for the entire crew. And Dad was asking if it wasn't too bad!

"Compared to what?" I groaned as I climbed up beside him. My back ached, I was sunburned, my hair was as stiff as straw and I was covered with insect bites.

"Compared to the fast-paced life of a modern teenager." He wheeled the van down the gravel road, a telltale cloud of white dust rising behind us. "And, incidentally, what's this with you and your mother?"

Dad was not one to waste time on small talk before getting down to basics. My obvious answer was, "Why?"

"That's what I'm asking. Why? Why can't you and your mother get along?"

I almost asked him the same thing, but I didn't think it was quite the thing to do at the very start of what was looking like a head-to-head with my father.

"Well . . ." I tried to stall. It was as hard to do with Dad as it was with Mom. "Nothing I do suits her. I can't even fold a towel to please her."

"Oh, I think you have it all wrong, Cricket. She's terribly proud of you. Take your score on the SAT. She's still talking about that."

"That's different."

"Why is that different?"

I remembered reading in one of Mom's books that a parent should never ask a child why, but that was the whole trouble. Parents never follow their own rules.

"I'm talking about something else." I watched the center line on the pavement slip by as if it were moving instead of us. "For one thing," I began again, "she doubts everything I do or tell her. She treats me like a ten-year-old."

"Sometimes you act like one, Cricket."

I didn't try to explain to him that sometimes I felt like a ten-year-old and other times I felt completely adult and that it was the adult that couldn't get along with Mom. That's the trouble with all mothers. They don't want their daughters to grow up. Look at anyone's photo album: oodles of baby pictures and pictures of starting to school, of the grade school play; then the pictures thin out and by the time the kid has reached sixteen the pages are blank, as if the mother somehow lost interest.

"You'll have to try to be more help to your mother." I kept wishing he'd quit calling her "your mother." It sounded as if he wasn't even related to her anymore. "She's under a great deal of pressure, you know, to get this new book started. You will try to make it easier for her, won't you?"

How could I promise? He was asking the impossible. I knew from past experience that if I didn't want to answer a question I either said that I didn't understand or I changed the subject. I changed the subject.

"You know, I'll sure be glad to get home. I'm really bushed." With that I curled up in the corner of the seat and pretended I was asleep for the rest of the way home.

9

MOM RUSHED OUT THE FRONT DOOR AS WE turned into the drive. She must have been waiting for us. At first I thought something awful had happened, because she didn't usually stand around waiting for people. People waited for her.

"You'll never believe what's happened," she called as she ran down the steps and across the lawn toward us.

"You had a phone call." Dad sounded pleased. Mom and Dad were like that. They could carry on an entire conversation without once revealing to anyone else what they were talking about. Mom had never said anything to me about expecting a call.

Mom gave Dad a big hug, and he whirled her around as if they hadn't seen each other for months.

"When?" Dad looked as thrilled as Mom.

"Tomorrow, if I can make it."

"You can make it. You've been half expecting it ever since the TV thing, haven't you?"

"Yes, but I can't believe it's really happening."

I stood in the drive, my bedroll in one hand and my

backpack in the other, wanting to scream, "Tell me what you're talking about," but instead I just stood there feeling completely invisible and unimportant. If they thought I was going to ask them anything, they were both mistaken.

"I'll bring my stuff over first thing in the morning. What time does your plane leave?" Dad turned to me. "Think you can stand me for three weeks?"

I guess Mom finally remembered she had a daughter, since she came over and took my bedroll and started for the house. "I'd love to take you with me, Tracy, but I can't. Anyway, you'd hate it."

I tagged along behind her, feeling like a neglected child. "What's the big deal?"

"The big deal," Mom answered with that parental patient tone, "is San Francisco, Los Angeles, Dallas, Miami, New York, Chicago. The grand tour of book promotion. Didn't I tell you about it?"

If she had, I hadn't listened.

"It'll mean living out of a suitcase, answering the same questions in every city and smiling all the time."

"I think that's great," I said, and meant it. No mother for three weeks! No grounding. Total freedom. Just Dad and me and no demands. Summer vacation was looking up.

"Take care of your dad," Mom said the next morning just before she climbed into the car to go to the airport. Then she turned, hugged me and whispered, "and be a good girl."

I think that must be a standard, built-in good-bye for all mothers.

I turned and started back up the walk when Mom rolled

down the car window and called, "And don't forget, Tracy, you're still grounded until I get home. After that we'll see."

Mom had a memory bank like a computer. At that moment I wouldn't have cared if she were going to be gone for six weeks.

Taking care of Dad was fun for almost two whole days. Instead of sleeping late, I got up and fixed him breakfast, which he didn't finish, dusted and vacuumed the house, which he didn't notice until I pointed it out, and made a couple of edible dinners for which he was late.

One thing that I discovered halfway through the first day was that caretaking was not a full-time job. Even if I dusted in slow motion, the whole downstairs didn't take more than half an hour, leaving a whole empty day stretching ahead. I watched the morning game shows on TV, the noon news, and the afternoon soaps and there were still hours left before Dad would be home for dinner.

Of course, when Mom said grounded, she'd meant only in the evening, but it didn't matter because there was nothing to do in the daytime either. Amy and her family had left for vacation. Stanley, even if I'd wanted to see him, which I didn't, was on a week's camping trip with some of the guys, and Mary Agnes, whom I'd tried to call in a moment of total depression, was on some kind of retreat for class presidents.

I was so bored that I even went grocery shopping, something that I hated and that Mom always took care of. But since she was gone, stuff like orange juice and milk and bread didn't appear magically in their appropriate places.

I took Mom's car. I figured that was okay since she'd more or less abandoned Dad and me; besides, going to a supermarket was bad enough without having to walk to get there.

The only reason I stopped to look at the bulletin board by the line of grocery carts was to postpone the inevitable shopping and choosing and touching and weighing and comparing. An archeologist of the future could reconstruct a fairly good idea of the town if he unearthed a grocery store bulletin board intact. There were the usual TVs for sale along with stereos, word processors, 1957 cars, and old playpens, and garage sales. I read through all the Lost Pets and the Wanted Baby-Sitters and then I saw, tucked down in the lower corner, Reader Wanted. The notice was typed neatly on the small business card of a Dr. Adrian Grantham. "For two weeks. 3 to 5, weekdays only."

I pushed my grocery cart down the aisle, wondering why a doctor would need someone to read to her and what could she want read? Medical journals, no doubt. I stopped by the pet foods to figure. Maybe I could make around ten dollars a day, that is if there weren't too many Latin words. That would amount to thirty-five or so dollars a week. I could have almost seventy dollars, maybe, by the time Mom got home, and even enough to buy a new bathing suit, after all.

Of course, just because the ad was still up didn't mean that the doctor hadn't already hired someone, but on my way back to the car, I memorized the address and decided to stop there on the way home. I didn't have anything more exciting to do and maybe, if I got the job, I could offer it as proof to Mom that I was "responsible." I could even help Stanley out with the money for his SAT, something that I hadn't gotten around to.

I missed the house the first time past because it was mostly hidden from the street by a double row of large old spruce trees. When I doubled back and pulled into the drive, I saw it *was* a house and not a doctor's office because there was no parking lot and no sign. For a minute before I punched the doorbell, I thought about turning around and getting back in the car. I really didn't have any overwhelming need for money. The bathing suit could wait. I didn't know anything about this doctor or what she wanted a reader for, and I wasn't sure if she'd even consider a high school kid for the job anyway. Then I remembered the empty afternoons stretching ahead and pushed the button.

It took a while, but finally the door opened and a man peered out at me. "I'm here about the advertisement," I said. "The one in the grocery store for the doctor. Is she in?"

He looked at me for a moment or two as if he were translating my words into some kind of more acceptable English, and I wondered if he was deaf or maybe just kind of occupying some kind of space of his own.

"You mean Dr. Grantham, I presume. *She* is *he,* which translates to *me.*" He must have decided that I was harmless because he took a couple of steps backward and motioned me into the hallway.

"I'm sorry," I said. "I guess I thought Adrian was a woman's name. What kind of doctor are you?" I knew he should have been asking the questions, not me, but I couldn't match the man in front of me with any kind of doctor I'd ever met. He was short and round and old, at least his fringe of hair was totally white, but his face wasn't wrinkled; in fact, he looked a little like a baby-faced Santa Claus without the beard and hair.

"I am a doctor of philosophy, my dear. One of a legion—a redundant legion of scholars—has been, presently are, would-be. A professor *emeritus,* who has toiled in the groves of academe, tasted its fruits and now, at last, is reaping the bittersweet rewards of his labors. In other words, in my previous incarnation, I was employed by the Department of English at our local university." His speech had lasted all the way down a hall and into a study, where he pointed to a chair for me and sat down behind his desk.

"Are you still looking for someone? To read, I mean." I wondered if he always used so many words to answer a question.

"I am not so much looking as listening. If my looking abilities"—he pointed to his eyes—"were adequate, I would hardly need a reader, now would I? I usually have a university student, but he left for the summer. As it is, I have been listening for someone who has a reasonable command of the language and whose voice does not sound like fingernails being pulled across a blackboard. Have you any idea," he went on, barely pausing for breath, "how many mumblers, eliders, and nasally impaired people are at large? All of them, evidently, under the impression that I should pay them for the painful experience of suffering their presence for two hours at a time. That is Monday through Friday for the next fortnight. You do know what a fortnight is, don't you? At five dollars an hour. Can you start tomorrow and what is your name?"

If the last five minutes had been any sample, the two-hour reading time would be mostly taken up with his talking, so he'd be paying *me* to listen.

"Tracy Spencer," I said. "And it all depends on what you want me to read. I mean, I don't know Latin or anything like that."

"Spencer. Spencer. Oh, of course. I know your"—I could feel it coming. I'd just walked into another of my mother's fans and he'd probably spend the rest of the time telling me how much he admired her books—"father. Reclaiming the native prairies and all that. Right?"

"Right. Sure, that's my dad, but how do you know I'll be able to read the kinds of things you want to listen to?" I wondered if I sounded as if I were trying to talk him out of giving me the job.

"Because, Miss Spencer, in the little time I've given you the opportunity to speak, you have not yet mispronounced a word, albeit they have been mostly of one syllable. Beyond that, you do not chew gum, nor fidget with your feet, nor twist at your hair. And what I want you to read is written in lucid English that an eighth-grader should be able to comprehend—at any rate it should be comprehensible to a high school student, which I presume you are, even though you have yet to say 'someone goes like' or insert a dozen 'you knows.' "

I couldn't resist. "You mean, you know, like I'd really enjoy reading for you. I mean it sounds like totally awesome."

He didn't exactly laugh, but he closed his eyes and made a little sort of sputtering noise that ended up in a wheeze. "I think," he said, "that we will have a satisfactory, if brief, relationship. I doubt that it will be awesome, but it may prove educational . . . for both of us." He stood up. "Tomorrow, then?"

"Tomorrow," I promised.

I announced my employment to Dad as he was finishing dinner that night, only an hour late. I was beginning to understand why Mom had quit cooking the elaborate meals that used to occupy her afternoons before she began writing books. Not that any of us went hungry, but about a year before the repotting, she'd begun making, during the week, something she called a moveable feast. I swore I'd start the same thing the next day.

"Grantham?" Dad almost choked on his cold tuna melt. "I didn't know he was still alive; he was *my* professor in freshman English. He must have retired years ago. I still remember his reading a kid's essay out loud to the class. The kid had written something about a 'chester drawers' in the corner of his bedroom. He didn't even laugh—he just launched into a lecture about idioms that lasted the rest of the period."

"He hasn't changed," I said. "He can still say ten sentences without breathing. And he knows who you are."

"Take the job, Cricket. Enjoy the good professor and giggle your way to the bank or wherever you're going with the loot." He pushed his chair back from the table. "I have to run back to the office. Be home around ten. You want to come with me or want to stay home?"

I didn't want to stay home, but sitting around Dad's office for the rest of the evening didn't exactly thrill me either.

"Oh, I'll stay home and go to bed early," I said. "I'll leave the porch light on."

About nine-thirty, Mom called. She did every night,

and I couldn't decide if she was homesick or if she was checking up to make sure I was home, observing my grounding.

She sounded a little disappointed when she found out Dad wasn't home and a little too happy when I told her about my job: "I'm so glad you've found something useful to do." I wasn't sure if it was a compliment or a put-down, but I gave her the benefit of the doubt and even asked about her last television interview. By the time she finished telling me, I felt as if I'd spent ten minutes with Dr. Grantham. She ended the way she always did. "Good night, honey. I love you."

"Sure," I answered. "Me too."

I turned on the porch light and headed for my bedroom. Maybe the main problem between Mom and me was that we lived in the same house; everything was so much easier when telephone wires stretched between us. I wondered if she felt the same way.

The next day, I appeared on Dr. Grantham's doorstep at one minute to three. He looked the type that placed importance on minutes. A lady—she introduced herself as Mrs. Lowden: "I clean and cook for the doctor."—answered the door and showed me into the study.

"Exactly on time!" He sounded surprised, as if he'd expected me to be late. "I thought we could start with a little essay by Aldo Leopold, one of my favorite writers. He's been gone for a long time, but I like the way he writes about things natural, wild, and free. Those are his words."

We sat, he tilted back in his desk chair and I in a straight chair over by the window that looked out on a backyard of plants and flowers, not in rows and individual beds, but random, as if someone had merely tossed out the seeds and let them take root where they would.

I could see why Dr. Grantham needed a reader. The print was so small in his copy of *A Sand County Almanac* that I had to squint now and then so I wouldn't lose my place. I tried my best to read slowly and distinctly, pausing at commas for a short breath and longer at the semicolons and periods. I tried to remember everything Mr. Jackson had told us in speech class, pitching my voice low and using the range of my voice so I didn't thump along in a monotone.

"The last word in ignorance is the man who says of an animal or plant: 'What good is it?' To keep every cog and wheel is the first precaution of intelligent tinkering. We have not yet learned to think in terms of small cogs and wheels."

He stopped me there.

"You see, we must save the pieces, because if you take apart a watch, you don't dare throw any part away, even if you don't understand where it fits. Man today keeps destroying his universe. How will men in the year 3000 ever know about us if we have destroyed all the cogs and wheels?"

"I see what you mean," I said, but I really didn't quite, so I went on and finished the essay.

"Can you read poetry?" He stood up and went over to a shelf and took down a thin green book.

"I think so." I didn't think you read poetry differently than you did anything else. The book was so thin I knew we could whiz through it in no time.

I read the first poem, about a middle-aged professor looking at some birds in January. When I finished, Dr.

Grantham, his hands pressed together as if he were praying, repeated the last line of the poem, in sort of a sad way, I thought, "What fools we are, we stoics!"

I waited for him to tell me to read on, but he didn't.

"You have to have lived, Miss Spencer, to have written that," he said. "Now go on."

The next one was about some castle in Wales, but when the poet told his friends about it they thought he was talking about cheese! It didn't make a whole lot of sense to me, but Dr. Grantham chuckled at the joke. I launched into the third poem:

Under a boil of clouds

"Stop right there! Always read the title of a poem. It contains the clue to the meaning without giving away the secret the poet is sharing."

I started again:

UNSEASONAL

Under a boil of clouds,
Heat's summer-simmer crowds
Inept, just-budding May.
Surprised, she gulps to say,
"Go 'way! You're much too soon.
Talk to my sister June."

Heat, lecherous and sly,
Leers as he whispers, "I
Mistook you for July."

This time I laughed. "I sort of like that one."

"I knew the poet. He'd be happy you liked it. He and

I taught here at the university. I always maintained a person had to be forty before he could write a good poem. He said seventy would be more like it."

We were halfway through "Soliloquy in Late Summer" when he stopped me. "That's enough."

"Don't you want me to finish the poem?"

"It's five. Mrs. Lowden will be bringing my dinner."

I was right. He was a minute man. He took a ten-dollar bill from his wallet and handed it to me. "See you tomorrow, then?"

"Yes, sir," I replied, taking the bill. "And thank you."

Now if Stanley didn't show up, I had the down payment on my suit at La Petite Miss. It was really a bikini—a bikini Mom said I couldn't have.

"You're not going to pay that much for something with no more material in it than a Kleenex."

But I was.

I should have known. With friends like Stanley, the future was never secure. That night, Dad had gone back to his office to work and I was about ready to go upstairs and wash my hair—it was a good cure for boredom—when the phone rang. At first I thought it was Mom, but when I answered, some strange voice mumbled, "That you? Come get me."

I thought it was someone pulling my leg until I heard, "Trace? Can you . . . come . . . get me?"

"Stanley!" I practically shouted into the phone. "Where are you?"

"Here . . . but I'm not sure . . . why . . . or how . . . I got where . . . I am." He was talking as if his mouth were full of mush.

"Can't you talk plainer? I can't understand you."

"I said . . . come get me . . . please?"

I hadn't heard Stanley cry since we were kids, but he sounded, now, as if he were going to any minute.

"Try to think straight, Stanley." I tried to sound like Mary Agnes. "Where is here?"

He didn't answer right away, but I could hear him mumbling something to someone in the background. "I'm at Orville's Gas Station on the . . . west corner . . . of Main Street." There was more mumbling and muttering and then, "In Maple Grove. Can you come . . . get me?"

Of course I could. Of course I would. Of course I did.

I left a note for Dad: "Gone to pick up Stanley," hoping the magic of Stanley's name would excuse my taking Mom's car at ten o'clock at night and driving nearly twenty miles down to a little wide spot in the road called Maple Grove. That's about all it was, a gas station and a main street.

The road was not unfamiliar. Grandma Ida's old farm was just off the Maple Grove road a mile or two. Stanley and I had often ridden our bikes down to visit her and Grandpa, but even a familiar road can seem strange when it's dark and you're driving alone. The filling station was closed when I reached Maple Grove, and Stanley was sitting outside on the curb, his head between his knees.

"Thanks," he mumbled as he crawled into the seat beside me. "Someday . . . I'll do . . . something . . . for you."

"I won't count on it, but you can do something for me this minute. What happened?" I made a U-turn in the middle of the one-block main street and headed toward home, wondering how I'd ever explain this little excursion.

"I'm not . . . sure. Honest. I think . . . maybe . . . I blacked out."

"How many did you have?"

"Only two. Maybe three."

"Two or three what?"

"I can't remember."

That's when I really let him have it. "You big Stupe! Have you ever had your IQ checked? Why can't you learn to drink like everyone else? Didn't anyone ever tell you to take it easy? Sip a drink. You don't have to guzzle one. Can't you learn when to stop?"

"I told you . . . it makes me feel good . . . usually." His voice sort of faded out, then in again. "If . . . people'd get off my back . . ."

"Don't pull that old I-got-problems stuff on me. We all have problems, but we don't crawl into a bottle to solve them. You think my life is all sweetness and light? And"—I paused for breath—"furthermore, I am supposed to be grounded and here I am at eleven o'clock at night dragging you home from somewhere you can't even remember where or how you got there."

"You won't tell, will you?" He sounded like a seven-year-old.

"Who's there to tell? And why should I tell? It's your problem, and if you mean will I tell your mom and dad, of course not. I'll drop you off at your corner, and you can walk the rest of the way. You can walk a half a block, can't you? Do you have your key? Or did you lose that along with your brain?"

"Don't need a key. I'll get in . . . the same way . . . I sneaked out."

I didn't ask how he'd do that. I didn't want to know. To tell the truth, I wasn't sure I wanted to know anything about Stanley. Ever!

We didn't talk much the rest of the way home. Stanley slumped over against the window and fell asleep—I thought—while I struggled to keep my speed down to within the legal limit. If a patrolman stopped us, at least one of us could pass the breath test.

I couldn't resist making one last parting shot as I dropped him off at his corner. "You know, Stanley. I think you have a problem. A big, fat problem."

"Thanks, pal," he drawled nastily. "I'll record your words of wisdom." And he slammed the car door so loudly I was sure it would wake the whole neighborhood.

I almost told Dad the truth the next morning when he greeted me with "What's this with Stanley last night?"—but I didn't. Instead, I covered for the birdbrain again.

"He needed a ride home," I answered.

"Oh. I didn't hear you come in."

That was because I'd been lucky. I'd turned off the headlights at least half a block away and coasted down into our drive and into the garage. Mary Agnes was a pro at that. I learned from her.

"It wasn't very late. You weren't home when he called. Neither were his folks. I didn't know what to do, so I took Mom's car. That was all right, wasn't it?"

"Sure. Sure." It was a loaded question, and I think he realized it as well as I.

At least I was off the hook as far as using Mom's car

without permission and breaking Mom's grounding rules, but I still had Stanley whether I wanted him or not.

For some stupid reason, though, I felt responsible for him. Why could some people drink and be all right while Stanley got completely looped on one drink—or so he said. I had to ask someone about it—to find out if Stanley really was on the way to being what we'd learned in grade school to call chemically dependent. But how could I ask someone without involving Stanley?

I knew what Mary Agnes would say: "Are you out of your little mind? Leave him alone." Amy wouldn't be any more help: "Relax! It's no skin off your teeth." I couldn't imagine going to his parents and saying, "Bob and Mavis, do you know your son is turning into a drunk? And that if you don't do something, he's going to kill himself or someone else or both?"

There wasn't anyone left but Mom. "What should I do, Mom? I think Stanley is a falling-down lush. He keeps getting drunk out of his gourd. He even blacks out on beer!"

But facts only confused Mom.

Who was I to turn to when there was no one left to turn to? Then I decided that maybe that was what growing up was: having to make my own decisions. So, I decided. I'd ignore Stanley and his problem. He was probably doing it just to show off. As Amy would have said, it was no skin off my teeth.

The next day, on my new job with Dr. Grantham, I read the front page of the morning paper, some more essays, all about the Peloponnesian (which I didn't know how to pronounce) War, which was surprisingly interesting particularly after Dr. Grantham explained what they were all fighting about, and of course several poems.

The third afternoon it was a Henry James short story, only it was terribly long for a short story and besides I had to take several breaths where there weren't even any commas in order to get through some of the sentences. After that we didn't read anymore, but Dr. Grantham talked.

The next day I read not only the front page of the morning paper but the entire editorial page as well, and we discussed that at length; in fact, that was all he had me read. That Friday, however, I walked into his study and he didn't have any books or magazines laid out and when I looked at him sort of questioning, he said, "We're not going to read today. Enough of sponging on other people's ideas. We will talk."

"I've never been paid to talk before." I laughed, and then wished I hadn't said it. When I looked at him again, I began to wonder if his eyesight was really so bad that he needed me to read to him or if maybe he was just an old man, lonesome for someone to talk to besides Mrs. Lowden, who came just in the afternoons.

"Talking is a form of reading, you know," he went on as if he hadn't heard what I'd said. "We talk so that we can read the other person's thoughts, values, beliefs. . . ." He paused and scratched his head where the baldness disappeared into a fringe of hair just above his ears. "My grandmother called it conversating. It's a marvelous word for it, far different from 'having a conversation,' don't you think?"

"Oh, yes," I agreed, wondering how much I had to contribute to the "conversating" to earn my ten dollars.

"You see, you young people today interest me. I'm

fascinated by the language you invent—the 'he goes' for 'he says,' the 'you know' and the 'did'n'—by your scheduled, mad rush of a life and all the allurements to buy and own that you must face. I don't suppose you can understand that, can you? Why an old man, having used up his eighty-four years, would be interested in all that."

"I understand, sort of." I was *not* holding up my end of the "conversating."

"When I taught at the university, they told us that adolescents had to face a number of developmental tasks in the process of growing up. They didn't know about such things when I was a boy—things like discovering identity, learning to be independent. Nowadays, young people not only have to accomplish all that, they have to come to terms with alcohol, drugs, and sex, all before they're old enough to recite their multiplication tables."

"I'm not sure, Dr. Grantham," I broke in, "that they insist on reciting those anymore, what with calculators and all."

"I try to imagine," he went on, looking up at the ceiling, "what it would be like to be young in today's world. Probably just as difficult as being old in today's world."

"How do you mean?" At least if he kept talking, all I had to do was make an inane comment now and then.

"We spend our lives learning to live. It's a time-consuming job, I can attest to it, but the thing that has me puzzled now is how fast time goes when you're young and how slowly it creeps by when you're my age. Which proves time is merely relative. Isn't that what Einstein was saying?"

I soon quit commenting and merely listened. It was as if he were reading to me, and it was interesting, I had to admit, mostly because no one had ever talked about the things he was talking about—or if they had, I wasn't listening.

"Life is growth. To grow, you have to learn who you *were,* who you *are,* and what you *will become*—in other words, the past, present, and future of yourself. You learn that only through communicating with others who mirror what you are. Shakespeare said it much better when he said the daughter is the mother's looking glass, and I suppose the son is the father's looking glass. That's beautiful, isn't it? Just think, you can look ahead and see mirrors endlessly multiplying. Some poet said that once. Can't remember who."

I decided to remember that mirror thing and think about it later.

He talked about a book he had read. "It's a book you should read as an adventure story when you're young; then again when you're forty to understand what it's about; and then as an elderly person to understand what old Melville meant."

I hadn't read the book. I think he said it was *Moby Dick.*

He talked about the danger of upsetting nature's balance and how he thought the only useless creature on God's earth was the box-elder bug: "It doesn't *do* anything. It doesn't eat anything, and nothing will eat it. It doesn't make any noise. It just crawls around and exists. Perfectly worthless."

I began to feel like a college class of one sitting in for his daily lecture.

He talked about all the other people in the world besides us and how we all should find beauty and meaning in worlds other than our own. "Nothing contributes more to pure ignorance than being locked into one's own experiences when there is a universe of differences to explore."

Sometimes I had to repeat his words over to myself to figure out exactly what he was saying.

Then he said something about how when he was young he used to know all the answers, but now there were so many new questions to be answered, and I thought about Stanley. I was almost ready to ask him what he knew about mixing beer and pot when he stopped in mid-sentence, looked at his watch and announced, "Time's up. You've been most patient, listening to an old man's ravings." He took out his wallet.

"I don't think you owe me anything," I said. "I mean, I didn't read or do anything to earn it."

"You listened." He held out the ten-dollar bill. "You will probably forget all this, but some day you will remember. That's what's so wonderful about the human brain. It remembers."

10

I HADN'T SEEN STANLEY ALL THAT WEEK, BUT he caught me one morning as I came out the front door on my way to see Mary Agnes, who had just gotten home from her leadership training gig.

"Hey, Trace! Hold it," he shouted as he came jogging toward me. "You have a minute?"

"No. But what's wrong now?" I knew the way he sounded that I was going to be taken in again.

"Nothing much." He wiped his forehead in the crook of his arm and grinned. Stanley had the most engaging grin of anyone I ever knew. I think that was part of the reason he could con anyone into doing whatever he needed to have done. "Wondered if you'd give me a ride downtown."

"What for?" I was *not* going to let him snooker me into any more good deeds for his benefit.

"I . . . I have an appointment."

I raised one eyebrow.

"Honest, Trace. It's important."

"I know. I know." I vowed, no matter what, I was not

going to let him borrow any more money from me.

"How important?"

"I have to appear in traffic court this morning. Got a ticket last night."

I felt my vow beginning to waver. "What for?"

"Speeding."

"In your dad's new car?"

"Noooo way! Dad won't let me drive that!" He turned and looked up the street. A couple of years ago, I might have thought he was embarrassed. "I was driving Jeff's car."

"Tell me all about it." I tried to sound sarcastically concerned. "And you're afraid to tell your folks. Was it just for speeding?"

"What else?"

"Could have been a lot of things—if I know you."

"Nope. I lucked out. Didn't even have to take a breath test. Anyway, I was only going ten over the limit."

I turned and started toward our garage, Stanley a step behind.

"It's going to cost me. Something around thirty-five or forty dollars. I'd get it from Mom, but she'd want all the dirty details."

"And I don't?" I slid behind the wheel. "Get in," I muttered.

"You going to stake me to forty dollars, maybe?"

"On one condition," I said, waiting for him to go around to the other side of the car.

"What's that?" He brightened.

"That you tell me why I'm such a sucker. You still haven't paid me the fifty bucks you've owed for I don't know how long. And it just occurred to me," I went on as I backed down the drive, "that for some reason I am always aiding and abetting you in all your dumb scrapes. Tell me why, will you?"

"Because I'm so charming?" He leaned over and peered directly in my face.

I refused to look at him.

"No, seriously, Trace." He sat back in the seat. "I'm just accident prone, I guess."

"Come off it, Stanley. You know as well as I what's wrong. Don't you know you're playing around the edges of something terribly dangerous?"

"Oh, spare me, Trace. I've had Mary Agnes on my tail all week. Don't you start."

"Okay. Okay." I waited at the stoplights to make a left turn. "It's your problem. Not mine. But why am I driving you down here as well as providing the money for your fine?"

"Because you're my friend." He reached over and patted my hand.

"No! You're wrong." I eased Mom's car into a parking slot. "Because I'm stupid! And I'll bet you still haven't registered for the SAT."

I waited in the car while he went in and paid his ticket with *my* hard-earned money—almost a whole week's worth of reading for Dr. Grantham, down the drain.

I dropped Stanley off at his house, and as I put Mom's car away I decided I'd had it. It was absolutely, positively the last time I'd help him out. Already he owed me eighty dollars. I actually thought seriously of going to his folks—of telling them what was going on with Stanley and that I wanted my money back—but if I did, I knew I'd lose not only Stanley as a friend, but Mary Agnes and Amy too.

I couldn't afford that.

If Mom had been home, I might have told her about my problem, but I wasn't sure she'd understand, anyway. Dad was out of the question. He'd go to Stanley's dad and the whole neighborhood would erupt. So I did what I always did when I didn't know what to do. I didn't do anything. I didn't even look up Mary Agnes.

That afternoon at my reading session with Dr. Grantham, I started out as usual with the front-page headlines from the morning paper, none of which interested Dr. Grantham. I turned from the national news to the local news to see if I could find something else.

"Local Youth Charged With Public Intoxication," I announced. Dr. Grantham didn't say stop, so I read on. "The thirteen-year-old's name was withheld, and he was paroled to his parents, who maintained they were unaware of their son's alcohol problem." I finished reading and swallowed.

"How sad," Dr. Grantham said, gazing out the window.

"Yes," I agreed. "He was only thirteen."

"Not the boy, although that certainly is sad enough. I mean the parents' not being aware. What an awful risk young people face when they start experimenting with alcohol . . . or drugs." He looked at the ceiling, and I knew I wasn't going to be doing much reading for the rest of the afternoon.

"We live in a society where social drinking is perfectly acceptable and accessible, so it's most difficult to convince a young person he shouldn't drink. But there are some—

like this young lad—whose brain chemistry probably is such that even the smallest amount of alcohol is addictive. Some little quirk in the brain, I guess. It is called Jellinek's disease because somebody named Jellinek proposed the theory that alcoholism was a disease."

"Does the person always know if she has it?" I used "she" instead of "he," but I had to find out if that was what Stanley had.

"Probably not. She knows she can't drink like everyone else, but she doesn't understand why she can't control it. Are there any young people in your school like that, do you think?"

"I don't know for sure. Well . . . Maybe yes. I guess so."

I didn't like the way he was looking at me. Did he think *I* was the one with a drinking problem? I guess it was more to protect myself than to help Stanley that I blurted out, "Well, you see, there's this friend of mine . . ." and I told him about Stanley. I didn't tell him Stanley's name, of course. I let him think we were talking about a girl.

"So this friend of yours. What makes you think she might be into something she can no longer control?" He leaned across the desk, his hands clasped in front of him.

"She doesn't know how to drink. She passes out. Once she blacked out and didn't even know how she got where she was."

"Have you tried talking to her?"

"She won't listen. She says she likes the way it makes her feel."

"And her parents?"

"They don't know."

"And you, of course, want to help her." He looked out

the window again. "She is someone who is very dear to you, no doubt."

"Well . . . yes. We've always been friends. We grew up together."

"I see. And I suppose you feel some guilt. Perhaps, in an innocent way, you have been helping her. I mean, perhaps providing excuses for her when she was indisposed, shall we say?"

If guilt was colored red, my face told him everything he needed to know without my answering.

"May I ask, have you talked to your mother or father?"

I hoped he didn't think that was the answer.

"Not yet." I secretly complimented myself at how beautifully vague was my answer.

"I think that is whom I would talk to first. You see, your friend needs help, and your folks would know how to go about finding the correct source."

"You mean I should . . ." I couldn't find the right word. I didn't think he'd appreciate "rat" or "snitch" so I tried, "Fink on her?"

He leaned back in his chair. "Sometimes, Miss Spencer, you have to do what may seem to be the wrong thing in order to do the right thing."

Just then Mrs. Lowden came in with some iced tea for us, and then I spent the rest of the time reading book reviews to him from some literary magazine.

During our last two sessions, Dr. Grantham never asked me anything further about "my friend." He was leaving for a month's visit with his daughter, and not only was Mom coming home that weekend, but Amy was returning from her vacation on Saturday.

* * *

Our house, when Mom wasn't around, was just a place to be when there was no other place to go, but the minute she swept in the front door, with Dad behind her carrying her bags, the whole house came alive. The phone began to ring. Dad hurried off to the supermarket with a list of groceries neither one of us had thought to get before Mom came home. She pulled up the shades in the living room, rearranged a chair over by the fireplace, sorted through her accumulated mail, stirred up a pitcher of lemonade and picking up three glasses said, "Let's sit out on the patio and talk. I'm so glad to be home."

I didn't say it. I should have said it. I was glad she was home, too.

"And everything went all right, didn't it, while I was gone?"

I should have answered, but I didn't. The last thing I wanted to do was talk about anything that had happened while she was gone. I needn't have worried. Mom wanted to talk—about her publishers, shopping malls, autographing books, and staying in hotels.

Dad came back with two sacks of groceries and announced, "We're having steaks on the grill." Mom's energy was catching. He'd never offered to grill when we were the only ones home.

The big surprise, though, came after we'd all eaten together out on the picnic table like a real family, when he said, "I'll do the cleanup tonight." I couldn't believe what I was hearing. I didn't think Dad even knew how to run a dishwasher.

By this time it was almost dark. Crickets were doing their cricketing and the hedge at the far end of our backyard was alive with fireflies. Mom was stretched out on the chaise longue, staring up at the stars that were just beginning to appear. As I watched her, I thought of Dr. Grantham's "mirrors endlessly multiplying" and wondered, if a daughter were a mother's looking glass, could I ever measure up to what she was seeing in her looking glass.

Then, as matter-of-factly as if she were commenting on the lovely evening, she said, "Sam has sublet his apartment for the coming year. His colleague Chris needs a place."

She hadn't said "your father." She'd said "Sam."

I couldn't resist. I felt so happy inside all I could say was, "Repotted?"

She burst out laughing. Mom had her polite "lady" laugh and she had her real laugh. This was her real laugh. "My darling Tracy," she said, wiping the tears that I think were from laughing, "there's nothing more dear to a writer's heart than to be read, but to be quoted is icing on the cake."

The peace in paradise lasted only until the next day. By that time, Mom had reestablished contact with all her friends, including Amy's mother and Mary Agnes's mother.

I knew something was wrong when I heard her hang up the phone with a decisive click and call from her study, "Tracy. Come here a minute."

I didn't answer, nor did I get up from the sofa where I'd been watching a rerun of "The Brady Bunch." I waited until she called me again and then I walked slowly into her study.

"Tell me, Tracy," she started, and I knew at once it was

going to be the third degree, only I'd had the third degree so many times I thought this would have to be the thirty-third. "Is there anyone you know who's been drinking to excess? Blacking out and passing out?"

I stopped halfway through the door. He'd betrayed me! Dr. Grantham had betrayed me! Here I'd trusted him without ever thinking he'd spread it all over the neighborhood. All I'd wanted was someone to talk to about Stanley.

"I was just talking to Mary Agnes's mother. Her neighbor's cleaning woman heard it from another cleaning woman who said that a high school or junior high girl was either an alcoholic or addicted to drugs, she wasn't sure which. And she said that the parents either didn't know or didn't care."

I tried to keep my voice from shaking. "Who's her cleaning lady?"

"I didn't catch her name. Why?" Mom looked grim.

"I don't know. I just wondered."

It was Mrs. Lowden and her iced tea that afternoon! She'd probably been listening outside the study door. At least it didn't sound as if she'd mentioned my name. With any luck, she wouldn't involve me, and if she did, I could always say I lied to Dr. Grantham, which would be true because part of what I'd told him *had been* a lie.

"Who do you suppose it could be, Tracy? Are any of the girls in your class involved in something like that?"

"Oh, Mom!" I tried to fake utter disbelief at the suggestion. "None of the girls I know would be that dumb."

"Someone in junior high, then? Do you really think that's possible?" Mom, the detective, was on the trail of an idea and I couldn't think of anything that would stop her.

I started back to the living room to shut off the TV. Mom followed.

"You know, if there's one bit of truth in all this, something needs to be done. It's like some kind of awful communicable disease; once an infection starts, it can spread everywhere."

I switched off the TV. I knew if I didn't escape immediately, I'd be in for a lecture that would probably end up as part of a chapter in her new book.

"Amy's home," I said, and headed for the front door. "She wants me to come over and see her."

Amy spotted me coming up her street and ran to meet me. I should have been tipped off that something was wrong. Amy seldom ran.

"We're in deep trouble." She grabbed my arm and whirled me around. "We've got to talk to Mary Agnes. Somebody told my mother there was a young girl around here who's a real lush and her parents don't even know it. So this morning she was baking and she found the rum bottle. It was almost empty. At first she accused me."

"You're kidding." But she didn't look as if she was kidding. "What'd you tell her—about the rum, I mean." I was glad Mom wasn't noted for her tortes or puddings.

"I told her one of the twins got into it and spilled it. They're good at that. Well, it could have happened. Then Mom asked me if any of my friends were into alcohol or drugs."

"And what did you say?"

"Well, I couldn't lie to my mother."

"Amy! You didn't. . . ."

"You're right." She was walking so fast I had to slip in an extra step every now and then to keep up with her. "I didn't. One of the twins got tangled up in our dog's chain, and I ran out to rescue her. When I came back, Mom had forgotten what she'd asked me."

Mary Agnes's mother answered the door. "She's up in her room watching some educational film on jungle animals. Go on up."

Mary Agnes wasn't watching an educational film on jungle animals. She was sprawled out on her bed watching a soap opera. "It's about time. I've been waiting for you two." She propped herself up on one elbow. "Which one of you weasels squealed on us and our little cultural exchanges?"

"Not I," Amy flopped down on the bed beside Mary Agnes, leaving me standing alone in the middle of the room, guilt written all over my face.

I didn't say anything. Instead I pretended a sudden interest in the angry words that someone named Trent on TV was shouting at a weepy, red-eyed blond named Laura. I knew their names were Trent and Laura because they shouted each other's names whenever it was their cue to talk. It really wasn't necessary because there wasn't anyone else in the scene except Laura and Trent.

"What about you?" Mary Agnes was using her putridly pure voice and looking directly at me.

I sat down at the foot of the bed and ran one finger around the circular design on Mary Agnes's new brass bed. She always claimed it was real brass, but it wasn't.

Stanley had me stick a magnet on it. He said if it stuck, it wasn't brass. It stuck!

"What *about* me?" I replied, hoping they wouldn't answer *that.*

Mary Agnes crawled off the bed and switched off the TV. "Only we three knew about our little cultural exchanges, so who's been spreading the rumor about some alcoholic right here in River City?"

"Stanley knew," I said, trying to defend what was looking like my indefensible position.

"The fish? He wouldn't dare fink on us. We've got too much dirt on him. Or would he?" Mary Agnes squinted over at me.

"Only under the direst of circumstances," Amy answered for me.

Mary Agnes was still looking at me. "Tracy Spencer! Did you ever tell anyone about our little rum and Cokes?"

"No," I said, and it was the truth. I would never have lied to Mary Agnes nor Amy. Never!

"It's all a big fuss over nothing, really. Everybody's got it all wrong." I started to explain and then I couldn't stop. It was strange. I couldn't talk to Mom or Dad about Stanley, and I could only hint to Dr. Grantham, but with Amy and Mary Agnes it was different. "It's really Stanley," I began.

"Stanley?" Mary Agnes almost shouted. "You mean he ratted?"

"No. He's the one the story's about. All I told him was that I had a friend who I thought was getting hooked on beer and maybe drugs and I wanted to know what to do because I was worried, and he assumed I was talking about a girl."

"Who?"

"Who what?"

"Who assumed?" Mary Agnes sounded like our school counselor again.

"Dr. Grantham."

Amy sat upright on the bed. Mary Agnes fell back on the bed.

"Who's Dr. Grantham?" This time Mary Agnes did shout.

It was late in the afternoon before I got through explaining everything that had happened with Stanley while they were gone: how I'd been a reader for Dr. Grantham, how I didn't know what to do about Stanley and about all the money he'd borrowed from me, and how I made up a fake story to ask Dr. Grantham for his advice. "We've got to do something," I pleaded.

"Hot Line?" Amy suggested. "We could call the Hot Line—if we didn't have to give our names."

"Tail him," Mary Agnes ordered. "When we catch him buying the stuff, we'll turn him in."

"Turn in Stanley?" Amy cried.

"Not Stanley! The seller."

"But we're not sure he's on drugs," I broke in. "Most of the time he wipes out on beer."

We couldn't come to a decision. None of us even suggested telling his folks. I thought of saying I could ask Mom, but I didn't. I knew what they'd say to that.

Before we went home, Mary Agnes said her folks were invited out for dinner that night, so why didn't we come over for a little "cultural exchange" and maybe we could decide what to do about Stanley.

11

I WAS BEGINNING TO AGREE WITH DR. Grantham and his theory of the relativity of time. It was simple. That was why January, February, and March crawl by and June, July, and August speed by. Already that summer the malls were advertising back-to-school bargains, and it was only the last of July and I hadn't begun to do all the things I'd planned to do during vacation.

I was thinking about all that as I walked over to Mary Agnes's house that night, when I heard a familiar, "Trace! Wait a minute."

Stanley jogged up beside me. If I hadn't known better, I would have thought he was a regular five-miles-a-day fanatic jogger with his sweatband across his forehead and matching sweatshirt and shorts—except the new white Reeboks gave him away.

"Don't tell me it's the new Stanley? Going out for track?"

"Maybe. But I saw you go by and I wanted to pay back

the money I owe." He pulled a wallet from his hip pocket. "Eighty dollars, isn't it?"

"With interest," I reminded him.

"Okay. Plus interest." I held out my hand, and he counted out four twenties and two ones.

"What happened? You win the lottery?" Maybe he'd finally settled down and gotten a job. Maybe I'd only been imagining things.

"No." He slipped the wallet back into his pocket. "Just picked up a little easy money last week." Stanley could be such a dork when he tried to act grown up, but why he thought he had to impress me was beyond my imagination. I did notice, though, there were more bills left in his wallet.

"Doing what?"

I don't know why I asked. I knew I wouldn't get a straight answer from him. Things had changed, and it made me sort of sad. Always before, Stanley and I had shared whatever was going on in our lives whether it was good or bad, but since he'd started running in the fast track, we didn't "conversate," as Dr. Grantham would have said. Instead, we small-talked our way around things.

"Dinky jobs here and there. Delivering pizza. Mowing lawns."

"Must have been some big lawns," I said, starting off for Mary Agnes's street. Stanley followed.

"And of course Dad pays me whenever there's stuff to do down at his office."

"You haven't been lost in Maple Grove lately, have you?" I half kidded.

"No way!" he shook his head. "That was weird, you

know? I can't figure out what happened. It's all blank, like a dream you can't quite remember."

"Stanley Prentice!" I stopped and grabbed his arm. "You mean to tell me you can't figure something out? It's the first time in your entire life that you've ever admitted anything like that. Why don't you go to the library and look up Jellinek's disease?"

"What's that?"

The truth was I *had* gone to the library and looked up about drugs and alcoholism, and what I'd read was awfully scary.

"Look it up for yourself," I said and went up the walk to Mary Agnes's house.

He stood there for a moment; then he turned and walked back toward his house . . . walked, not jogged.

Anyone would have thought that the rumor of a neighborhood teenage druggie would die out after a couple of weeks or so, but it was not the case. Mom, who usually dismissed a juicy piece of neighborhood talk as "pure gossip," suddenly shut down her word processor and started making the rounds like a precinct cop, seeing if she could pick up any evidence of teenage drug misuse or alcohol abuse. It was upsetting. Just when things began to look normal again with Dad around, Mom had to upset everything. Before, I could count on knowing exactly where to find her—in her study punching chapter after chapter into her processor—but now I never knew where she was. She'd pop in at the weirdest times and sometimes she didn't even make it home for meals.

"Sam," she announced one morning at breakfast. "What would you think if I were to organize a group to fight drug use here in our neighborhood?"

Dad looked up from his morning paper. Mom didn't often ask his advice on any of her projects. "What kind of a group?"

"Concerned parents. I was talking with some of the other women around here, and one of them told me about the town where her sister lives. They organized such a group, and they've practically cleaned up the entire town of pushers and peddlers and teenage beer parties."

I winced. All I needed my senior year was to have a crusading mother out to spoil everyone's fun. I didn't know any pushers, and there were only a few guys like Stanley and Jeff and Brent who didn't know how to handle a kegger.

"We thought we'd put an announcement in the paper. We'll call ourselves Concerned Parents Against Drugs: CPAD. We're scheduling our initial meeting at Mavis Prentice's in their rec room."

I nearly choked on my last spoonful of Cheerios. In Stanley's rec room!

Dad folded his paper and tossed it on the table. "Are you sure you aren't overreacting? I mean, there's nothing wrong with your group idea, but look around." He gestured toward the window. "Do you really imagine that any of the kids here are dumb enough or disturbed enough to get involved with drugs? It's not like we're living in a ghetto. These kids get their kicks from spending money on clothes and video games, right, Cricket?" He sounded as if he was trying to convince himself.

It was a rotten question no matter which way I answered, so I tried to switch the focus. "It sounds great, Mom, but it would be kind of a waste of time with your new book and all. Besides, they do all that kind of stuff at school. I mean, we have assemblies and guest speakers and reformed druggies. They even passed out buttons last year—'Just Say No' buttons."

I didn't tell her that most of the kids had inked in *w*'s after the *o.*

She looked at Dad and then at me and took a deep breath. "If there's even one kid around here who's using anything, there's someone who's selling, and someone else who is supplying that seller."

"You have a point." Dad downed the last swallow of his coffee and stood up.

"You two are so oblivious to the problem," Mom said, "that you probably wouldn't recognize a pusher if he offered you free samples."

Dad grinned at her. "I have to get to the office, but if I run into any dirty old men lurking on street corners, I'll give you a call. Otherwise, I'll see you around five." He headed for the door. "And as far as the cleaning person is concerned, she probably has an overactive imagination. Too much TV while she's pushing the vacuum."

I certainly hoped Mom would drop the whole subject. All my concern about Stanley seemed silly, really. I had to admit there were some *real* druggies at school; everyone, all the kids anyway, knew who they were, mostly because of the way they dressed and who they hung out with. Stanley didn't look like any of them. And as for the beer, that's all it was. Just beer and mostly just on weekends.

"Tracy, you've never . . ." Mom was still sitting at the table, but she was frowning now. "I mean I'm sure you wouldn't, but you've never tried any drugs, have you?"

I couldn't believe she was actually asking me such a question. Of course I hadn't. It was such a dumb question that I didn't even answer. Instead, I shook a little line of sugar on the table, rolled up my napkin and *pretended* to sniff. That was a mistake.

Instead of laughing, Mom stood up so fast that she almost knocked her chair over. "You're as bad as your father and his silly joke about dirty old men. Don't you understand that this is serious? You can laugh about the story as much as you want, but if there is even one grain of truth in it, somebody has to do something." She started out of the kitchen and then turned back. "I'm going to be in my study and you"—she paused and took another deep breath—"can clean up the mess you've made on the table."

Great! Mom had been home for just three days and already she was ticked at Dad, furious with me and about to launch herself into a cleanup campaign that would have half the kids in school laughing themselves silly. All because I'd been dumb enough to talk to Grantham. Why couldn't she be like other parents who didn't get themselves involved in their kids' lives?

I cleaned up the table and wondered if I should call Stanley and warn him that the vigilantes were on the prowl. And they would be, because if there was one thing I did know about my mother it was that once she got hold of an idea, nothing short of a natural disaster could make her let go.

I didn't call him, though. Amy, Mary Agnes, and I spent the afternoon at the pool showing off our new bathing suits. They didn't seem too worried about the idea of Mom's concerned-parents group, because as we all agreed, no one we hung out with, even Stanley, was really into anything heavy and the worst that could happen would be a couple of meetings and the whole thing would be over before school even began.

How wrong could I get? I had forgotten the power of the press. We dropped Amy off first at her house, but when Mary Agnes pulled up in front of my house, there were Mom, Amy's mom, Mary Agnes's mom, and . . .

"Do you see what I see?" Mary Agnes groaned. "That can't be Stanley's mother, can it?"

It was, and standing beside them on the porch steps was Connie, our local TV reporter, talking to Mom while a TV cameraman recorded the entire affair. "CPAD, Concerned Parents Against Drugs, is holding its initial meeting this evening at the home of Robert Prentice. And tell me, Mrs. Spencer, what do you hope to accomplish this first meeting?"

"We will be enrolling members and planning our strategy for the year." Mom sounded like an army sergeant preparing her troops for an attack. "Our aim is to rid our neighborhood and school of drugs and provide a safe and nurturing environment for our children."

I didn't move to get out of the car. "Do you realize," I began, "it'll be shown on tonight's news?"

"And do you realize that if we get out of this car, our mothers are entirely capable of using us as examples of what needs to be nurtured?" Mary Agnes took her foot off the brake and we coasted past our driveway and on down the hill.

"What are we going to do?" I asked, sure that before another week went by our mothers would have us going door to door passing out petitions.

"I'm not sure." Mary Agnes was looking grimly serious. "It's not as if they were *promoting* drugs. It's just so . . . embarrassing."

"So public, you mean," I added.

"So unnecessary," she agreed. "And it's not as if we lived in Chicago or something. I mean, it's a good cause and all, but why does it have to be—"

"Our mothers?" I finished for her.

"I'm sure of one thing." Mary Agnes turned the car around and headed back for Amy's house. "We have to give Amy the six o'clock news alert."

Amy's reaction was typical. She screamed, not loudly enough to wake the twins from their afternoon naps, but with plenty of sincerity. "How can they do this to us? It's not like Mothers Against Drunk Drivers, or something. That's a *real* problem, like robbery or murder. And why did they have to go out looking for a problem?"

"Well," I suggested, "there *is* Stanley."

"The only thing wrong with Stanley is that he drinks too much beer and smokes a little pot. It's not as if he's into coke or crack or dust." Amy stopped and looked at us. "Is he?"

"Of course not," Mary Agnes said after a few seconds. "Even Stanley couldn't be that dense. But he got us into this, and he is going to have to get us out. After our mothers appear on tonight's news, all the other kids in school are going to think we're either finks or druggies. Maybe you can think of a way we can skip our senior year."

None of us could, of course, and before we could make any real plans the twins woke up and started crying. Amy's mother's car pulled into their drive, and we agreed that if Amy could get away later we'd meet at my house, watch the news together and try to figure out how to use Stanley to bring CPAD to an early but honorable end.

When Mary Agnes finally dropped me off at home for the second time, Mom was on her way out the door. She must have forgotten that she'd been mad at me that morning because she gave me a one-armed hug. "Trace, I've some errands to run and then I'll be at the Prentices', but I should be home around nine. There's something in the refrigerator for your dinner and your dad called that he has a dinner meeting, so I'll probably be back before he is." She was almost out the door when she added, "Oh, and honey. Be sure to watch the local news at six. I think we do have things started."

Later that evening, we turned off the TV news and looked at each other in horror. This crusade wasn't going to be any two-week wonder. They were planning to blanket all the schools. They had battle plans drawn up that would have stopped the Vietnam conflict before it started.

"You know what's going to happen, don't you?" Mary Agnes looked almost frightened.

"No," I said.

"They're going to conscript us to pass out their pamphlets. I just know it. Can't you see us standing on street corners?"

"I won't be able to," Amy grinned, a feline grin. "I'll have to take care of the twins."

Mary Agnes ignored her. "Next thing will be drug testing in gym class. And it's all Stanley's fault, the wart!"

"We've got to do something!" Our talk was going nowhere, and I wanted a definite plan of action.

"All right." Mary Agnes sounded as if she were back

in command. "Solution number one: Stanley becomes the sacrificial lamb. Either he tells his parents or we do."

"About the beer, but not the pot? Or about the pot, but not the beer? Or both?" Sometimes Amy could be very precise.

"All or nothing," I ventured, feeling a twinge of guilt.

"Of course, if we mention the beer, he may mention our cultural evenings," Mary Agnes pointed out.

"Let's hear solution number two," I suggested.

"I know," Amy piped up. "Make Stanley swear he'll never take another drink or drag!"

"I don't think that will do it," Mary Agnes said. "I get the feeling that The Mothers are primed to reform the entire public school system."

"So, what's solution number three?" Amy looked first at me then at Mary Agnes.

"Rum and Coke?" Mary Agnes asked with a shrug, and then shook her head. "I guess that's a bad suggestion tonight. Well, one thing for sure. We never, never, never lend Stanley any more money. At least that way we won't be contributing to anything. How do we know he wasn't using the cash to buy pot?"

"No more money," I agreed. "So besides that what have we decided?" The last time I'd seen Stanley's billfold, it didn't appear as if he were exactly hurting for money.

"All right. Before we make a final decision," Mary Agnes said, "we owe it to ourselves to talk to Stanley."

I thought maybe we owed it to Stanley, too, but I said, "I've already talked to him."

"Me too," Amy yawned.

"Well, for that matter, so have I," Mary Agnes went on. "But it's time all three of us confront him."

"With what?" I asked.

"With the fact that his experimenting and fooling around is screwing up everything for us and everybody else." Mary Agnes was angry. "And if he isn't careful he's going to get us into trouble."

"What trouble?" Amy wasn't yawning now. "We don't do drugs, do we?"

"Of course not," Mary Agnes snapped. "Rum isn't a drug. It's nothing but fermented molasses. But when the Mom Squad gets into full swing, we're all going to be under surveillance."

"What do we do if we're asked about Stanley?" I wasn't sure I could lie convincingly enough to convince Mom about him.

"We say we don't know." Mary Agnes smiled her innocent best.

"That's sort of a lie, though, isn't it?" Amy asked.

"Borderline, maybe, but if we say we don't know we're merely asserting our constitutional right of not saying anything that might incriminate *us.*"

So we swore not to reveal anything—anything about what we'd been doing or anything about what we knew or thought we knew about Stanley. It didn't feel quite right, but I went along with it anyway.

12

IT WASN'T LONG BEFORE PACKAGES BEGAN to arrive. Almost every day, sometimes twice, the UPS truck pulled up in front of our house, and Mom's study slowly filled with cartons of what she called educational materials. When she wasn't sorting, stacking and piling stuff in her car for distribution, she was attending meetings, talking on the phone or writing letters to places that would send more boxes of stuff to be sorted, stacked and distributed.

Finally, one morning, she called to me, "Do you suppose you could help me? I want to get these packets ready to hand out to the junior high schools as soon as school begins."

She had stacks of pamphlets, dittoes of newspaper articles, medical statements all pointing out the effects of drugs and alcohol—piled up and extending across her desk and over two card tables.

"Now, if you would walk around this way and pick up one from each pile and slip them all into one of these manilla envelopes, it would certainly make my job easier."

I wasn't doing anything that morning, so I started in, picking off the packet stuffers and piling up the filled envelopes into big cardboard boxes that lined the other wall of her study: *What Every Teenager Should Know About Alcohol, I'm Not That Bad Yet, Facts About PCP, Don't Start, Then You Won't Have to Quit, Just Say No.*

"Mom," I said, starting on my twenty-fifth tour around the desk and card tables. "They've got all this stuff in junior high already. At least they had it when I was there and it hasn't changed much."

"They might have had something like it, but this is all new, updated material and it's full of terribly important information." She sounded so earnest that I almost felt sorry for her.

"It may be important, but no kid is going to read it unless somebody's going to give them a test on it the next day. They could probably fake the answers, anyway, just from listening to television. I know you're trying to do something good, but kids know most of this stuff by the time they hit third grade." I finished packet number forty and slumped into a chair. It was amazing that someone as smart as my mother could be so dumb when it came to kids.

She stopped whatever she was doing on the word processor and looked at me as if I'd stuck a pin in her favorite balloon. "Are you trying to tell me all this is a waste of time? Or are you just embarrassed about our distributing these to the schools?"

Maybe she wasn't so dumb about kids, at least not when it came to *her* kid. I decided to ignore her last question and concentrate on the first one. I wasn't sure she'd understand. "Look, Mom, it's really simple. Maybe it's not exactly a waste of time, but it doesn't *do* much of anything except for the kids who wouldn't use drugs or alcohol in the first place. Maybe for them it's—what do you call it—reinforcement, but they already agree before they even read it."

"What about the others? Do you mean they won't read it or that they won't understand?"

"Oh, they might read it, and they'd probably understand it, but they wouldn't care."

"Tracy, that's an enormous generalization that you couldn't possibly back up statistically." She was so smugly adult that I began to get angry. After all, I was only trying to do *her* a favor. It took all I could do *not* to give her one specific statistic who lived about two blocks away and was named Stanley Prentice.

"Mom," I said, trying to sound the soul of patience, "you've forgotten how kids work. They don't believe everything they read. And anyway, when it comes to this stuff—alcohol and pot and junk—they're just seeing what's it really like. Just trying it for fun."

"What about you?"

She caught me completely off guard on that one. I thought a minute and then began, very carefully. "If I really wanted to, I probably would. Try it, I mean." Mom had a way of making me say more than I intended, so I hurried to add, "But I don't want to. See, I'm one of those kids I was talking about—one of those who already agree with what this stuff is saying." I hoped Mary Agnes was correct about rum being only fermented molasses, and that it didn't qualify as a drug.

I started around the tables for what seemed like the hundreth time, getting more and more ticked off. I wasn't sure whether it was the complete futility of what we were doing or that unshakeably right tone Mom kept using.

"The problem with you is that you think you're invulnerable. I don't mean just you, Tracy, I mean kids in general. You never believe that some things are too dangerous to experiment with." She sounded as if she were talking to a preschooler.

I thought about pointing out that *she* was the generalizer, except that she'd probably ignore the comment. Instead, I stuffed the last envelope and said, "And the trouble with you and all the rest of CPAD is that you're *not* kids; you're just one more bunch of adults telling us what we've already heard." I couldn't resist, so I added, "I don't mean just you, Mom. I mean people in general."

She didn't answer. She switched her word processor back on and started punching the keyboard as if she were erasing our whole conversation.

I started to leave. She looked up. "Would you mind taking these boxes of packets over to Mavis Prentice? You can take my car."

"Sure," I answered, for she was already laying out more pamphlets to be stuffed into a new pile of envelopes. She helped me carry the boxes out to the car. She didn't say anything more, and I didn't, either.

Mom must have called Stanley's mother, because as I drove into their drive Mavis Prentice was standing in the door and Stanley was coming down the walk to meet me.

"Going in for junior high brainwashing?" He winked.

"No, smart neck. Dry cleaning," I mumbled. "I'm beginning to think it's parental therapy." After the futile exercise in trying to make Mom understand the basic facts of life, it felt good to talk to someone who, at least at the moment, was functioning on my wavelength. "How's life on your home front?" I waved at his mother and turned on my brightest smile.

She waved back at the same time that Stanley, laden with two big boxes, said, "What life? They've suddenly discovered that their only son is a vulnerable teenager at the mercy of a dissolute world." He started up the walk. "How about giving me a lift downtown after I dump this? I need to meet a guy and our car is still off limits."

"Sure. Why not?" I figured Mom was too busy processing words to notice if I was gone for an extra half hour.

"Let's drive out to the Pits first, if you have time," Stanley said as he slid into the seat beside me and carefully fastened his seat belt. "The kid I want to see might be out there, and it would save us a trip."

"Okay," I agreed, mentally adding another half hour to my errand for Mom. "I think Amy and Mary Agnes gave up on the pool and headed out there this morning. If you want to stay, they'll probably give you a ride back if you can get them out of the water."

With the T-top off Mom's car and the sun shining and school still several weeks away, all the problems of the summer disappeared like the bits of cottonwood fluff drifting through the early afternoon air. And Stanley, sitting beside me, his eyes closed and his face turned up to the sun, didn't look at all like the blank-eyed kid I'd picked up at an empty gas station in nowheresville.

"How did you con your parents out of those?" I asked, pointing to his obviously new shoes that must have cost at least eighty-five dollars, even on sale. "And that shirt?"

Usually Stanley went around looking like something left over from a garage sale.

"It's part of my new image. Like it? My parents take this," he reached down and patted his left foot, "as positive progress through my developmental stages."

It was like talking to the old Stanley, the one I'd grown up with, the one whom Amy, only last year, had admitted she might even go to the Senior Prom with if he ever could be coerced into asking her. I felt like stopping the car and hugging him—dorky old Stanley. We'd been wrong all the time—Mary Agnes and Amy and I. There was nothing wrong with Stanley. He really had been fooling around, just experimenting.

By the time we got to the Pits, he had me laughing so hard I had trouble keeping the car on the road. He started with a perfect imitation of our mothers at a CPAD meeting and ended pretending to be a junior high kid suffocating under piles of the packets we'd delivered to his mother. That's when I decided that instead of the old Stanley, this was a new improved speeded-up model.

Amy and Mary Agnes had come and gone, so I sat in the car while Stanley went looking for the kid he was supposed to meet. The gravel pits looked a little like a midwest version of ocean beach in the afternoon sunlight. The water was deep and very cold farther out, but next to the shore that had been scooped out and leveled off, it was warm enough for swimming. The only problem was chunks of concrete pilings scattered across the bottom, left over from the time the Pits were worked.

Stanley soon came loping back. "Mission accomplished," he said, tossing a paper bag on the floor.

"Thanks a lot, Trace. You've brightened my day. I'll put it in The Book."

"Where to now?" I asked as I pulled out of the Pits and back onto an honest-to-goodness road.

"Drop me off uptown. Wherever." He settled back, rolled down the window and rested his head against the seat back.

"What's in the sack?"

"Nothing. This kid borrowed some of my best tapes. You know—Madonna and a couple Tiffany and the New Kids on the Block. I've had a hard time running him down to get them back."

It never occurred to me to doubt his explanation. Any kid knows you don't get that specific when you lie.

"Did you know, Stanley," I said, "we were really worried about you this summer. Do you realize that practically every time we've seen you, you've been drunk or stoned or both? You were getting to be a real drag."

For a minute he looked as if he was going to get mad and I felt a little guilty for bringing the whole thing up. Then he started laughing so much that I began to laugh too, even though I hadn't said anything funny.

"Don't worry, Trace," he finally said. "The whole secret is control. All you have to do is figure out how much of what. It's kind of like how much cheese you want piled on the pizza. Get it?"

I didn't get it. "I don't think it's quite the same. Unless you're allergic to cheese. Some people are allergic to alcohol. It's true, you know," I went on, hoping that I didn't sound like Mom giving a lecture. "Drinking anything is like playing Russian roulette, except that there aren't any empty chambers in the gun."

"Stick with pizza, Trace," and he started laughing again. "You don't know anything about—" He stopped laughing and grabbed my knee. "For Pete's sake, Trace. How fast are you driving? We just passed a radar trap. There was a cop at that crossroad!"

I looked down at the speedometer and groaned. I was doing fifty-five in a forty-five mile zone.

"What do I do?" I slammed on the brakes.

"Well, don't stop, for cripes sakes! Just slow down and try not to act guilty." He reached down and shoved his package of tapes farther under his seat.

I slowed down to forty-two and drove as carefully as if the road were coated with ice. I could feel my heart beating clear up in my throat. "Fasten your seat belt," I ordered, and glanced in the rearview mirror. They were coming—the flashing lights—and the siren—getting closer and louder by the second.

I glanced over at Stanley. If ever there was terror personified, he was it. His hands were shaking so that he could hardly click the seat buckle in place, and his face had turned a funny shade of puce.

"What's with you? I was only speeding. Maybe he'll just give us a warning. With luck."

The police car was directly behind us now, so I pulled over on the shoulder, shut off the motor, rolled down my window and waited.

"Whatever you do, don't say anything. Let the fuzz do the talking and don't go into detail. Just answer yes or no," Stanley whispered not turning his head, but staring straight ahead so that anyone in the rear would never have guessed we were talking.

"Good afternoon," the cop said. Even Stanley did a

double take. The cop was a woman—a petite, pretty, smiling woman who reminded me a little bit of Dad's office-mate, Chris. "May I see your driver's license, please."

I dug in my purse while she stood pad in hand, pencil poised. She took my license and returned to her car.

"Shall I say you are sick and I'm rushing you to the doctor? You look sort of sick."

"Don't say anything!" he practically shouted. "Just count yourself lucky that all we get is a speeding ticket."

"Why?" I looked over at him again. "What are you so scared about? We were only ten over the limit."

He didn't have a chance to answer, for Ms. Fuzzette was back. "Did you realize you were exceeding the speed limit by ten?"

"I guess so," I admitted, trying to look casual but repentant. "I guess we were talking and I wasn't paying attention and—"

Stanley gave me an elbow-thrust in the ribs.

"Good to see you were both wearing your seat belts. May I see the registration on this car?"

Registration! I almost panicked. What did she think? That we'd stolen the car? I remembered how Dad had kidded Mom when she first got the car new. "Every cop on the beat will be laying for you—a red T-top and all."

"Registration," I said sort of under my breath to the tongueless Stanley beside me. "Where would it be? What color is it?"

"Green, you dum-dum. In the glove compartment," he muttered.

She took the registration, checked my driver's license again and looked first at me and then at Stanley.

"Would you mind stepping out. We've been instructed

to run a breath test on any young people coming off the Pits road. A new organization here in the city, the CPAD, is instigating the practice in a concentrated effort to crack down on drunk drivers."

I would have gladly disowned my mother at the moment. The way Stanley rolled his eyes I knew he would not only agree to disowning all mothers but he would have divorced his on the spot, if that had been possible.

We passed the breath test. She handed back my driver's license, the car registration, and a pink slip of paper. We got by with nothing but a warning!

"Thank you." I tried to smile, but my face was stiff. Stanley exhaled a big "Whew!" as I eased Mom's car back into traffic and drove toward home with one eye on the speedometer. I glanced at Stanley and noticed that his face had turned from puce to a chalky gray. "Are you okay?" I asked. "You really look sick now."

"I'll be fine in a minute. Must be too much sun." He reached in his pocket and popped something into his mouth. "Salt pills," he explained. "You'd be surprised what they can do."

I was surprised because by the time I dropped him off downtown he was talking full speed again and acting as if the whole police thing was some kind of wonderful joke. I figured that with *his* driving record, he was just relieved that I was the one who got the warning ticket.

"Thanks again, Trace," he said, getting out of the car. "Whoops!" He reached under the seat and pulled out his sack of cassettes. "Almost forgot. I'm supposed to pass these on this afternoon. Trading them for a couple of old Grateful Dead tapes. Be careful driving home." He grinned at me and headed down the sidewalk.

Slowly and carefully, I pulled away from the curb and started back to the house. The warning ticket didn't worry me; Mom would never find out about that, and I wasn't about to volunteer the information. What I couldn't figure out was Stanley's new-found interest in music.

13

THE NEXT MORNING I WAS COMING DOWN the stairs, hoping Mom had remembered to pick up some frozen orange juice. She was so busy with CAPD that her grocery shopping left a lot to be desired. Dad was long gone to his office and Mom had left for the airport to meet some guest speaker who was to speak that night at the CPAD meeting.

"Anybody home?" someone called from the front door.

I hurried down to the hall, and there, of all people, was Grandma Ida, her purse dangling from one arm and a carry-on bag from the other, trying to shove two large suitcases through the front door.

"Grandma!" was all I could say before she flung her arms around my neck, her purse clipping me on one side and her carry-on bag banging me on the other.

"Now don't start asking questions like 'How'd you get here?' or 'Why didn't you let us know?' or 'Why all the luggage?' The answers are in order: I took a night flight and a taxi. Question two, if I'd let you all know, you wouldn't have let me come, and finally . . . I forgot what the last one was."

"Why all the luggage?" I prompted her.

"Oh." She looked down the hall. "Are you the only one home?"

"Yes. Why?"

"Let me have a cup of coffee first." She started for the kitchen. "Have you had your breakfast?"

"Not yet. I just got up." I followed her through the dining room and into the kitchen.

"You see, Tracy," she said as she pulled down the coffee can, "I'm tired of Arizona." She peered at the printing on the coffee can. "Don't tell me all your mother has is decaffeinated!"

"I guess so. So you're going to stay with us. I mean, you are, aren't you?" It sounded all wrong, but I meant it to sound like a welcome.

"Until I get settled. I'm moving back on the old farm. The cropland has been rented, you know, but the house has been vacant." She opened the refrigerator door and studied its contents. "Any oranges?"

"Orange juice." I pulled open the freezing compartment. Mom had remembered. "I'll mix up some."

"Don't bother. At my age I don't go in for concentrates. I want the real thing. Just skip the orange. Where'd you say your mother was?"

"She had to pick up a guest speaker for her CPAD meeting tonight."

"What's CPAD? Part of her research?" She popped two slices of bread into the toaster. "What do *you* eat for breakfast?"

"Nothing much. I guess I'll just have a diet Coke." I

reached in the fridge and pulled out a can. I couldn't see any use mixing up a whole pitcher of orange juice if no one but me was going to drink it.

"What do you mean a diet Coke! That's no breakfast. You'll rot your teeth." She poured out a glass of milk and set it before me. "Try that while I fix you some French toast."

As a French toast chef, Grandma Ida was superb. She finally sat down to drink her coffee. "I read once that the stuff they use to decaf this coffee is worse for a person than the original caffeine. That's so often the case. Cure's worse than the ailment."

"What about the rest of your stuff? Your furniture and all?" I wasn't interested in cures and ailments.

"Coming by van. In a few days."

"But Grandma, I thought you loved Arizona and your new condo and all your friends."

"My friends out there have forgotten how to laugh. You know they say a good laugh adds two hours to your life, and I'm getting to the place where I can use those hours." She set her cup down. "And I miss my old neighbors: Wilma and Evelyn and even Bertha. I never could really stand Bertha. She always rubbed me the wrong way, somehow, but I miss her anyway. The trouble was, out there, I really didn't get to know anyone that I cared a fig about. And people you don't care a fig about don't seem real. Nice, but not real. Like paper dolls. One dimensional. Old friends are so comfortable, like old worn-out sofas. They fit around the edges."

"What are you going to do with your condo?" I asked, but before Grandma could answer, Mom shouted from the hall, "What's all this stuff by the front door?"

"Tracy's running away from home," Grandma shouted back as Mom strode into the kitchen and, upon seeing Grandma, leaned up against the counter with a "Oh, Moth-er!" that sounded exactly like me.

"What on earth are you doing here?" Mom finally asked, leaning over and giving Grandma a half kiss on the cheek.

"Having breakfast." Grandma smiled over at me.

"I know. But what a surprise. Why didn't you let us know you were coming?"

"Question number two," Grandma said to me, barely moving her lips. "It wouldn't have been a surprise then, would it, Dotty?" There was just the least little bit of an edge to her voice. "Sit down and have a cup of coffee." As if she were in her own kitchen, Grandma went to the cupboard for a cup and poured it full of coffee for Mom, whose neck was turning a blotchy red.

"But Mother," Mom began. "Are those your bags?"

Before Grandma could answer, I jumped in. "She's tired of living in Arizona. She's moving back."

It was not a wise thing to do. I should have left it to Grandma to break that news.

Mom half choked on a swallow of coffee and looked up at Grandma. "Is that right, Mother?"

"That's right. I sold the condo. I'm moving back." She took another sip of her decaf.

"Oh, Mother! You didn't!" Whether Mom knew it or not, she was sounding more like a child than a mother; in fact, she was not only sounding like me, she was saying the same things I always said when *she* did something unbelievably dumb.

"She's moving back to her farm," I said, feeling like a referee.

"Oh, Mother. You can't be! How can you be so stupid?"

It was suddenly very quiet. It was strange. I could feel what they weren't saying to each other.

Finally, Grandma stood up, walked slowly over to the sink, rinsed out her coffee cup and left the room. Mom had done the very same thing to me once, when I told her she was getting to be a tiresome nag. Mom had gone into her study, shut the door and left me standing looking exactly the way she was looking now.

"I shouldn't have said that." She sounded as if she were apologizing to me.

"I'll take her bags up to the guest room. She came in on the night flight, you know."

"No, Tracy, I didn't know. I didn't know anything about anything. I can't understand Ida's doing something like this." Mom was losing her cool, something she rarely did.

"She misses her neighbors," I tried to explain.

"My bluebirds too, Dorothy," Grandma called from the other room. Obviously, she'd been eavesdropping. "And my chickens, the oak grove, snow, clean air, sky that never ends and . . . and I miss . . . all of you."

Mom looked up at me, set down her cup and hurried into the dining room. I headed for the hall and Grandma's bags. I didn't think the two of them needed the third generation around to offer any further explanations. All I heard, as I started up the stairs, was Mom's "Oh, Mother," but the way she said it almost made me want to cry—not because it sounded prickly but because it was full of warmth and . . . I guess you could call it . . . understanding.

As I set the bags down in the guest room, I thought about what Shakespeare had said about daughters being their mothers' looking glasses. Mom was definitely a mirror image of Grandma Ida, but then I thought that as a daughter around Grandma Ida, Mom acted strangely like me. It was like Dr. Grantham had said: mirrors endlessly multiplying.

I vowed never to have a daughter. She would probably turn out to be like me!

When I came back downstairs, Grandma and Mom were sitting out on the patio, planning what had to be done that next week before the van arrived from Arizona. "I sold most of my furniture," Grandma was saying. "There wasn't a comfortable chair in the lot. Is your father's old leather chair still up in your attic?"

It was, I knew. Dad could never talk Mom into getting rid of it, although every spring she vowed she would.

"And would you believe, Dotty, I sold that cracker box of a condo for nearly half again what I paid for it!"

They both laughed. They were friends again. I guess that's what being friends amounts to: laughing together. It had been a long time since Mom and I had laughed together. It wasn't my fault, though. She hadn't said anything funny for as long as I could remember. But for that matter, neither had I.

"We can talk more after I have a little nap, Dotty. I never could sleep on a plane." Grandma started for the stairs, Mother following.

"I hope you understand, Ida. It was such a surprise, your coming. A shock, really. I mean at first when you announced you'd sold your condo. It certainly didn't sound like the reasonable thing to do, at your age and all." Mom was still trying to apologize for saying Grandma was stupid.

"That, my dear, is why I got out of Villa Acres. I was getting *too* reasonable. Every day the same. Every hour the same. Here on my farm, every minute is different. You live from one breath to the next. A breathless breath, at that." She patted my arm as she started up the stairs. "At least my bluebirds will be happy to see me."

Mom looked at me and shrugged. What else was there to say?

That night, after dinner, we all drove down to check on the farm. "It's been vacant for the last few months," Grandma explained, "but Wilma and Evelyn and Bertha are coming in tomorrow and we're going to clean the place up."

I hadn't been out to the farm since Grandma had moved off, but as we drove into the yard, everything looked familiar. How many times, as kids, Stanley and I had spent the entire day visiting Grandma and Grandpa, riding my Shetland pony, Peaches, down across the ravine and into the oak grove that made up the border of the farm. Then in the spring, we used to help Grandma Ida clear out her bluebird nesting boxes that she had scattered all along the west-line fence. "We have to keep checking them," Grandma used to tell us, "to keep such intruders as sparrows and starlings from taking over the houses before the bluebirds get back."

We inspected Grandma's house, the garage, the chicken coops, the big machine shed, now empty of its huge combine and tillers and tractors, and finally the old barn. Dad pulled open the upper half of the stable door and looked in. "Ida, we could stage a dance in here. A welcome-home dance."

Mom was still looking around in the garage, and for fun, I pushed open the bottom half of the stable door and stepped in. The smell of dry alfalfa hay still lingered as I walked over to the stall where I had always kept Peaches. I remembered the wonderful tangy smell of her leather saddle and the feeling of complete freedom and control I used to feel as I galloped down the lane out to Grandpa's fields.

In Peaches's stall, it was not an odor of alfalfa hay nor of leather that hung in the air, but a strange acrid smell of something once sweet gone sour. The floor had been swept clean and boards piled one upon the other to provide a bench of sorts. In the middle of the stall were candles, matches, numerous beer cans, and an ashtray full of clips and ashes.

I didn't have to think twice to figure out who had been there and when. So this was where Stanley hung out . . . in my grandma's barn. If Grandma Ida ever found out, she'd have the county sheriff down in a minute and the place under twenty-four-hour surveillance at once. I started to stack the boards against the wall and hide the candles and the rest of the paraphernalia; then I stopped. Why was I protecting Stanley? He was using me—and Grandma Ida's barn—and I, like a dummy, was still covering for him.

I looked around the barn again—the barn where he and I had spent so many afternoons playing in the haymow and swinging on the hay rope that hung from the rafters—

and vowed I'd had it. I'd tell Dad what I'd found. On second thought, maybe it would be easier to tell Mom. On third thought, I'd tell Grandma and let the sheriff pick Stanley up. For the moment, I decided on none of the above, for I heard Mom calling, "Come along now, Tracy. We're going out to check on the bluebird houses. Grandma says she's afraid we've had intruders."

"Intruders!" I cried. "Wait a minute! I've got to tell you something!" But by the time I reached the door, the three of them were heading down the lane to check on *bluebirds*!

14

I WAS THROUGH WITH STANLEY. I WAS NOT going to help him anymore, but it was much easier to vow not to do something than it was not to do it. After all, I had to tell him that Grandma Ida was back and that she and her friends were going to be out at the farm, and that he'd better not plan on using Peaches's stall anymore for his fun and games. Grandma Ida might not catch on, but nothing escaped Bertha.

I tried to call Stanley as soon as I arrived home, but his mother said he was over at Mary Agnes's watching a horror movie on the VCR. He wasn't. Mary Agnes hadn't seen him for a couple of days. I was going to look him up first thing the next morning, but Mom caught me before I could escape.

"I told Ida you would drive her out to the farm this morning." It wasn't an order, but it was one of those requests mothers make that you know is a demand to be carried out, with the "or else" only slightly veiled.

"Do you want me to stay and help you, Grandma?" I

asked, knowing full well that she and Evelyn and Wilma and Bertha didn't want any kid around to spoil their day.

"No," Grandma answered. "And you won't have to bother to come after me. One of them will bring me back. I suppose you'll be spending the day writing, Dotty?"

Mother looked up from the morning paper. "No. I've been rethinking this latest book and I . . . well, I don't know. I'm not sure I'm capable of writing it."

It was the first time I could remember that Mom had not been completely sure of everything.

"What did I tell you, Dotty, last spring when you and Tracy came out to visit? Remember I said no one is capable of understanding daughters, least of all mothers?"

"I know," Mom answered, "and you were right, as usual." And she didn't say it sarcastically, the way I might have.

"What's so difficult about daughters?" I was being serious. "I would think writing about them would be a snap."

Grandma started out to the kitchen. "That's because you've never been a mother."

"Then what are you going to write about, Mom?" I was beginning to feel that I was to blame, somehow, for her giving up on daughters. "You've got to help yourself to something."

"I'm thinking of researching a different *D:* Drugs."

"Drugs instead of daughters," I offered. "And it won't upset your alphabet then, will it?" I really didn't mean to be cute.

Mom looked at me sort of funny. Sometimes it was hard to interpret her expressions, but I had learned, in such cases, to smile back.

"It will concern alcohol abuse as well as drugs and will stress the importance of educating our young people on the consequences."

I wondered if Mom had been measuring her rum bottle.

"So hurry back with the car, Tracy. I have some important things to tend to this morning."

"Are you ready, Grandma?" I called.

Grandma came out of the kitchen with a pail full of cleaning accessories and a broom. "Can you get the vacuum for me, dear?"

I loaded the car, and we started for the farm.

"Your mother is a bit annoyed with me," Grandma confided as I backed the car out of the drive. "And I don't blame her. I did something I shouldn't have done."

I couldn't imagine what it could have been other than leaving a faucet running in the downstairs bathroom—something that was so easy to do that Mom had posted a warning sign on the mirror.

"You mean leaving Arizona?" I asked.

"No. No, of course not, though I suppose I should have warned her." She fiddled with the crease in her perfectly pressed slacks. "I interfered. Your grandfather would have said I was suffering from nose problems."

"What did you do?"

"I asked your mother to explain this business of your father's moving out of the house and then moving back in again."

"You mean the repotting?" I suggested.

"Repotting!" she sputtered. "Repotting can be a messy business and sometimes plants die in the process. Fortunately, that didn't happen to you in this case, so I'd say you come from pretty hardy stock."

"She explained it, then?" I asked.

"She started to, and then I decided it was none of my business. It's the hardest thing a mother has to do—to let go—to let children live their own lives, make their own mistakes, suffer their own consequences."

I couldn't have agreed more.

"Somewhere along the line a mother has to stop being a mother and become a person. Drive a little slower, Tracy. I want to look at the crops along here."

I slowed down to please her. A blue Camaro, sporting streaks of jagged yellow lightning on its sides, zoomed past us with a swoosh that rocked Mom's car.

"Somebody's always in a hurry," Grandma complained.

"When would you say," I said, steering her back to our conversation, "a mother should stop being a mother?"

"When the daughter stops being a daughter and becomes a person. Look across there. Isn't that the most beautiful sight you've ever seen?"

It was a soybean field bordered by cornfields.

We turned off the blacktop onto the gravel road that led to the farm.

"This mother-daughter thing is crazy, Tracy. There will come a time, I don't want it, but inevitably it will come, when Dotty will feel that she needs to mother *me.* You see, the roles reverse, and the mother becomes the child to be cared for and the child becomes the mother doing the caring. But not yet!" she said brightly as I stopped the car and she pushed open the door. "Not yet by a long shot. Now help me in with this stuff and get on with your own life and forget all this nonsense I've been talking."

The other ladies were arriving as I pulled out of the lane

and onto the gravel road, but I hadn't gone more than a quarter of a mile when I glanced in the rearview mirror and there was the blue Camaro again. I stopped at the stop sign before pulling back onto the blacktop, and it was practically nudging my back bumper. I had never seen the car before, and as I rolled on up to fifty-five, it hung right with me.

Have your fun, I thought, and slowed down to forty-five. The Camaro did the same and followed me into town, down my street and when I turned into our drive, it came to a stop in front of our house. I got out of the car and started for the house, pretending I wasn't aware that the car had been following me.

A loud blare from the car horn made me look, and there was Stanley, tanned and handsome in white shorts and shirt, posing like a magazine ad beside the Camaro.

"How do you like it, Trace? I just got it."

"From where and how?" I cried, and ran across the lawn.

"From Dad. He promised me if I'd get the SAT out of the way before school starts, he'd let me have my own car. Pretty sporty, yes?"

"Beautiful!" I exclaimed. "If not ostentatious."

"Of course it has a few miles on it, but look." He opened the door on the passenger side. "Hardly any wear on the seats. Five on the floor, too."

"No overdrive?" I kidded.

He half laughed. "You don't forget anything, do you?"

"I try."

"Well, try harder, Trace."

It wasn't the time or the place, but I didn't care. I had

to know for sure. "It was you, wasn't it, Stanley, using Peaches's stall? You and who else?"

"Oh, that." I seldom could get to Stanley, but this time he looked sort of surprised. "That was a long time ago. I'm through with all that stuff." He threw out his chest and put his hand in his shirt front in a Napoleonic pose. "Straight-arrow clean, Trace. From now on. Honest!"

"Promise?"

"Would I lie?"

I refused to comment. Of course he would lie. Any kid would lie for a blue five-speed Camaro with spinners and lightning-yellow streaks down each side.

"I'd give you a ride," he said, climbing behind the wheel and rolling down the window, "but I'm late already. A bunch of us are organizing the traditional back-to-school senior bash. A picnic."

"A picnic!"

"It's a measley little job, but someone has to do it. Anyway, it's good for my image."

"You mean a picnic-picnic with wieners and buns and stuff like they always have?" I was beginning to believe Stanley and his "straight-arrow clean."

"I thought maybe potluck." He switched on the ignition key and the Camaro coughed, sputtered and roared to a start. "I'll let you know when."

"Where are we having it? Speaker's Park?" I envisioned a bonfire in the city park and all of us seniors sitting around roasting wieners or marshmallows and singing as the fire died down and the stars came out.

"The Pits! Where else?" He laughed, shifted into first,

made a tire-squealing U-turn in the middle of the street and shouted back, "Gotcha, didn't I?"

The rat! I don't know why I was so angry. I was always being taken in by Stanley. I guess everyone else was, too. If he just weren't so clever, so handsomely cute, so amusing, so likeable . . . so lovable . . .

"I'm back," I called to Mom as I came in the back door. "And did you *see* Stanley's car! A blue Camaro!"

Mom came out of her study, arms full of official-looking file folders. "I haven't seen it, but Mavis said they'd bought one for him. I hope your excitement doesn't mean that you'll expect one next."

"No way," I answered. "Why bother when Mary Agnes has one?"

"At least that's one thing we can agree on," Mom said, but she was smiling, so I didn't get ticked. She stacked the folders on the table by the door and turned toward me. "I'm not so sure we'll see eye to eye about the senior back-to-school party."

"What do you mean?" I asked, wondering how she could have already found out about what Stanley had just finished telling me.

"At our CPAD meeting, someone mentioned that it's going to be out at the Pits instead of in Speaker's Park."

"Really?" Someone in our senior class had a *very* big mouth. "That's a neat idea. It's still plenty warm enough for swimming." I waited for her to tell me that the Pits were off limits, at least for me.

"It's not that I don't trust you, Tracy, and I know it's a tradition. . . ." I waited for the "but." It didn't take long. "But it's not school sponsored, and you can't tell who'll turn up in a situation like that."

"Oh, Mom! Be real. If everyone in town knows where the party's going to be, what could possibly happen? I mean, there's no way anyone is going to show up with a keg or anything." I didn't add that at any official school function any time during the year, there were enough bottles of booze and cans of beer tucked away in car trunks to give *all* of Coolidge High a pleasant glow.

Mom didn't look convinced. "Well, I suppose you're right, in a way. I won't tell you that you can't go. . . . I just hope you'll be very, very careful." She picked up her folders and headed for the door. "I'll be back later this afternoon."

I couldn't believe it. We'd gotten through the whole discussion without an argument. Maybe she was finally learning that I was old enough to make up my own mind about things. Strange, though, I didn't have the slightest desire to attend the senior bash at the Pits. One time at Zumwalt and one time at the Pits was enough. The whole thing was really quite juvenile.

The next week was Grandma Ida's week. Everything else went on hold: Mom's CPAD as well as her new book on drugs, Dad's save-the-prairie-biomes project, and my social life, which never did operate on a very high intensity level. All was set aside in getting Grandma settled back on her farm, and that left only one week before school started again.

That last Friday night of vacation, I wedged myself into a corner of the backseat and stared out the open window, watching telephone poles flip past as if they were being yanked on a string, and wondered why I'd agreed to go along with Mary Agnes and Amy to the stupid senior bash.

"What are you so uptight about?" Amy peered at me from the front seat. "It's just another party."

She was right. It was just an ordinary evening at the end of summer when kids were caught between wishing vacation would never end and wanting to be back in school for another year before encountering what most of us were sure was the real world.

"Then why are we going?" I argued.

"What else is there to do? I suppose we could go to the mall and scope the latest back-to-school stuff that we can't afford to buy."

Both alternatives sounded boring, so I didn't say anything more and tried to listen to the conversation going on in the front seat. Mary Agnes was explaining why she absolutely refused to take the senior Great Books course even though Mr. Perkins, her counselor, insisted that it would ruin her whole college career if she didn't.

"So I told him I was thinking seriously of the Peace Corps and that something like advanced auto mechanics might be a lot more useful."

"The only auto mechanics I know are Fud Slaven and Mike Warren. And they are definitely *not* advanced."

Normally I would have laughed, but Mary Agnes suddenly sounded silly and Amy was talking like a snob.

"Looks like everyone is here," Mary Agnes said as she pulled off the road and started to back into a rutted lane that led into a cornfield. "We'll park here, and if things get dull, we can leave."

There was a rustling of cornstalks, and before Mary Agnes could switch off the motor, Stanley stumbled out of the cornfield, ran up to the car and jerked open the door.

"Cops!" he gasped, as he climbed into the backseat

beside me. "They're raiding the place. Get out of here!"

I'd never seen anyone's face absolutely white; Stanley looked as if someone had actually pulled a plug and let all the blood drain out of him.

Mary Agnes maneuvered the fastest U-turn in automobile history, and we barreled down the dirt road in a cloud of topsoil dust.

"Take . . . the next . . . right . . ." Stanley ordered. His mouth moved a couple of times before the words came out, and when they did, they were so careful I was almost sure he'd rehearsed them in his head before he spoke. He looked over at me. "It's not what you think, Trace."

"How do you know what I think?" I decided to wait for two more minutes or one complete sentence from him, whichever came first, before I opened the door and pushed him out.

"You probably think . . ." he began, and then started over. "You think I can't handle things. . . ." It wasn't as if he stopped talking. It was more like listening to something run down—air going out of a tire or a whistling teakettle when you lift it off the stove.

"What happened?" Amy loosened her two-handed grip on the dashboard and turned around.

"I don't know. State troopers all over . . . had kids taking Breathalyzer tests . . . doing body searches, even."

"Body searches! What for?" It was one of my more inane questions. I knew the answer without asking.

"Drugs, stupid." He leaned back and wiped his face against his shirt sleeve. "I had to get out of there . . . I mean, I had a little pot with me. There's no big deal with that. See, you always know how much of what is going to make what kinds of things happen . . . like . . . if you have a headache, you take an aspirin or two and it goes away. Right?"

Wrong, I thought.

"Right," I said, "if you say so, but the rest of the world thinks it's pretty dangerous. And I don't mean aspirin."

He sat up, leaned forward and looked around. "Turn right when you hit the blacktop." Then he settled back and grinned a big, almost normal Stanley grin. "See? I know what I'm doing."

"I'm glad *you* do, Stanley." Mary Agnes was on the verge of sounding nasty.

"No. I don't mean the pot. It's the other stuff . . . I can't figure out. I mean . . . I'm sort of scared." He lowered his voice, as if he thought someone else might hear him. "I can trust you all, can't I?"

That's probably the worst question in the world. If you say no, obviously the other person is going to stop talking. If you say yes, then you're promising something that you may not want to promise.

I compromised. I didn't answer. Stanley didn't notice.

"What other stuff?" Mary Agnes sounded scared now.

"The booze . . . beer . . . like it'd be awfully easy . . . I'm scared sometimes that maybe I'm . . . that I'll be . . ."

"A drunk?" Mary Agnes suggested. "Well, then don't drink! Or if you have to, stick to just one beer." She sounded like a repeat of a commercial for some television station.

"That's what I'm talking about. I haven't figured out how! I tell myself I'll just have one beer with the guys—just for fun, you know—and then the next thing I know, I'm blotto and can't remember anything." He sat up abruptly. "Here. Let me off. I'll walk from here. That way you guys won't get into trouble."

"What do you mean?" Mary Agnes almost shouted. "We're clean. We didn't even get there."

"Maybe you're clean, but I think the cop who was chasing me recognized me."

"What did he have on you?" Amy was interested now.

Stanley reached inside his shirt and slid The Book across to me. "Keep this for me, Trace," he whispered. "What did he have on me?" Stanley repeated for Mary Agnes's benefit while I slipped the small notebook into my jeans pocket. "I don't know. Probably because I ran."

"Where along here is here?" Mary Agnes kept looking into the rearview mirror as if she expected to see someone tailing us.

"I'll show you the place."

The place was the road leading down to Grandma Ida's farm.

"How are you going to get home?" I don't know why I was still worrying about Stanley. It wasn't quite dark yet, although the sun had gone down behind Grandma's oak grove.

"There's a guy I know who lives close to here. He'll give me a ride home."

15

WE FINISHED WHAT WAS LEFT OF THE EVEning walking aimlessly around the mall and talking about how lucky we'd been not to have arrived at the senior bash on time.

"You have me to thank for that," Amy said as she stopped to gaze at a shop window full of shoes.

"I don't know why," Mary Agnes broke in. "How many times did you change your clothes while we were waiting out in the car for you?"

"Only three times. Anyway, it saved our necks, didn't it?"

Finally our conversation switched to the one subject that we were all thinking about and that no one wanted to talk about—Stanley.

"Why was he so scared?" Mary Agnes asked. "If he had just a little pot on him, he could have dumped it somewhere."

"Maybe he did," I said, pulling my shirt down over his book in my hip pocket.

Amy turned from the shoe display. "Do you think

maybe there's something really wrong with him?"

"I think so," I said. "Don't you?"

Amy didn't answer right away; then she asked, "You can't really get hooked on pot, can you?"

"People can get hooked on anything—peanut butter, crossword puzzles, skateboards—you name it." Mary Agnes was not being flip.

"Maybe we could talk him into seeing a counselor or something when school starts . . ." I suggested, my voice sort of drifting off.

None of our ideas went anywhere, maybe because none of us could believe, or none of us wanted to believe, that the Stanley we'd always known was into something he couldn't handle. That kind of thing didn't happen to someone like Stanley. We finally gave up and went home.

It was a lousy way to end a summer vacation.

I was sure Mom would be up and I expected her to be waiting in the living room or kitchen with Dad at her elbow ready to do a double repeat of graduation party night. I was wrong.

They were in her study laughing at some ancient movie rerun on TV, and when I stuck my head in the door, the only thing Mom asked was, "How was the party?"

"I don't know." It was easy enough to answer, and I was glad I could tell the truth or at least most of it. "We never got there. We decided to scope out the mall instead. I think we've outgrown parties at the Pits."

That part was totally true. After what had happened that night, I never wanted to see the place again, and I was pretty sure Amy and Mary Agnes felt the same way.

Dad applauded. "Hope you mean it."

"Sam, I think we've done it!" Mom reached over and hugged him. "We may have raised a potential adult." She peered past the TV set at me. "Just kidding, Trace. You've always been a potential something."

She was still laughing when I said good night and headed upstairs. As I got ready for bed, I pulled The Book out of my pocket and placed it on the dresser and wondered why Stanley had given The Book to me, instead of to Amy or Mary Agnes, and what was in it that was so important that he couldn't hang on to it himself.

The more I thought about it, the more curious I became; in fact, I couldn't get to sleep for all my wondering. Several times I got out of bed, turned on the light and reached for The Book; but I couldn't quite make myself read what was in it, probably because I didn't want to find out that what *was* in it was really *there.* I decided I'd ask Mary Agnes and Amy whether they thought I should see what was in it, but I was pretty sure what they would say and I sort of agreed: what we didn't know wouldn't hurt us.

Mom's CPAD had run an ad in the local paper about substance abuse and included a printed form that you could clip and sent in to the editor. You didn't have to give your name or anything, just the name of someone that you thought was mixed up with drugs or alcohol. I'd cut it out and hidden it in my dresser drawer, but I couldn't make myself write in Stanley's name.

Around midnight, I considered calling one of those nighttime talk shows for advice or the hot-line number that was always being flashed on TV, but how could a stranger understand Stanley?

At two o'clock I still wasn't asleep, so I gave up, switched on the light and opened The Book. The pages were filled with dates, names, and numbers.

Rich T.	*I owe*	*1 six-pack*
Scoop G.	*I owe*	*5th V*

Some pages were all "I owes" which changed to "Owes me" with dollar amounts. I flipped over more leaves and there was an "I owe" for ninety dollars and *my* name. Further on, I found Amy and Mary Agnes neatly noted, but I wasn't sure for what. I didn't see ten dollars for the SAT anywhere. I recognized most of the rest of the names, too. Besides Jeff and Brent and Boyd, there were several girls in our class and a lot of kids from Coolidge who were in sports or music or drama, and a lot of straight arrows whose names were always on the honor roll.

I couldn't figure out the little initials Stanley used after some names; I guess I didn't want to, because I knew that whatever they stood for, our names—Amy's, Mary Agnes's and mine—were part of some kind of bookkeeping that involved a part of Stanley's life that I didn't want to know about.

I stuck The Book under my mattress, crawled back in bed and shut off the light. For the first time I understood how much Stanley had been hiding from me. It was past four in the morning before I stopped thinking and fell asleep.

Mom was on the phone when I came down for breakfast the next morning. Seeing me, she said good-bye to whomever she was talking to and hung up. From the look on her face I couldn't tell whether she'd been listening to good news or bad.

"You won't believe what's happened," she exclaimed, unfolding the morning paper.

"You were nominated for the Pulitzer Prize," I answered.

She held up the front page. "Agents Stage Raid." She read the words aloud as I stared at them. "The article says that the state drug and narcotics agents received an anonymous tip about drugs and illegal alcohol. Last night at the Pits! Oh, Tracy, I'm so glad you decided not to go there."

I stumbled toward the refrigerator. "Anyone arrested?"

"It just says 'a number of high school students.' They can't list names. All those kids are underage. Listen, though—the police found what they call small quantities of drugs ranging from marijuana to something they think may be cocaine. It says that more arrests are pending."

That could mean that Stanley was "pending." What about Amy, Mary Agnes, and me? No one had seen us, but we'd helped him get away. I poured my untouched orange juice back in the pitcher and stood by the sink, looking out the window, trying to figure out if we could be guilty of aiding and abetting. Or maybe Stanley hadn't done anything more illegal than the rest of the kids; he'd just managed to get away with it.

"There's an editorial, too," Mom went on. "It suggests that the area around the Pits be fenced in so it can't be misused again." She put down the paper and sighed. "I wonder why we always wait for the worst before we try to solve a problem."

"Me too," I said, remembering the emptiness of Stanley's face the night before.

"At least we looked ahead. The march was planned before any of this happened."

"March? What march?" All I could think of was "a number of high school students" walking, linked together, on their way to the police station.

"It was Mavis Prentice's idea. I guess I forgot to tell you. CPAD is going to march against drugs and alcohol. Next Saturday. We're involving the civic organizations and the schools."

"What good will that do?" The thought of Stanley's mother innocently tromping all over town as a Concerned Parent while he was, more or less, a fugitive made me feel a little sick.

"It will show that we care, that everyone cares about what's happening in our community." She stopped and looked at me. "Why are you making that face?"

"I didn't know I was. I guess I was just thinking about parades—homecoming parades, Fourth of July parades, centennial parades. I mean, who's going to watch unless you have bands and those men who drive little cars around and throw out candy to the kids?"

"This is different. This is serious. If even one person thinks about why we're doing it, the whole thing will be worthwhile." She looked so sincere that I almost felt sorry for her and all the rest of the parading parents.

"Yeah, I suppose you're right," I lied. "Is Dad going to be marching, too?" I hoped that he had an urgent need to go back out to the prairie-research area and hunt for mugwort or thistles or diseased weeds—anything that would demand my help.

"Sure, at least part of the way. And I thought perhaps Mary Agnes could help make signs and that you and Amy could . . ."

"I'll take care of the twins," I said, before she had a chance to volunteer me for something that would result in my utter humiliation. "Amy will do anything as long as it doesn't involve serious movement."

"Then there's Stanley," Mom began. "He's getting in touch with people who've promised to be part of the march. He'll drop off a list later this afternoon."

I collapsed in a kitchen chair. Stanley must have decided that the cop chasing him hadn't seen his face after all. Or else he thought the whole bust was such a joke that pretending to help organize an antidrug march was even funnier. Either way, it made me mad.

"Mom," I said, "there's something I want to tell you."

"Yes?" She looked up from the paper.

My anger evaporated as quickly as it had begun, and I couldn't finish the admission I had thought about making. I'm not sure what stopped me. It might have been because she wasn't my friend. She was my mother. So I said, "I'll go talk to Mary Agnes and Amy about making the signs."

"Okay, Trace. I should move, too. A lot has to happen before Saturday. We're getting together this morning to make final plans for the parade. Do you suppose you could fold those fliers there in my study when you get back? Stanley, you know, will be distributing them this afternoon."

"I suppose I could." It was a mindless sort of job that I usually tried to weasel out of, but that morning I didn't have the strength to argue. I was well into folding the second-hundred stack of fliers when, over the hum of voices from the living room, I heard Stanley's mother say, "We were worried for a while, but having his own car has made such a difference. He's becoming more outgoing, more extroverted. For a while he seemed such a social loner."

Stanley would have loved it—"a social loner"! It was a perfect oxymoron. And the two parts of Stanley didn't match any better than his mother's words—the half that we'd all lived with for sixteen years and the other half that listed names and secret deals in a little black book. That was the part that frightened me, because if he really was using drugs and selling drugs, he had to be buying them somewhere, too.

LOCAL YOUTH KILLED
DRUG DEALING SUSPECTED

Stanley Prentice, sixteen-year-old honor student at Coolidge High, was discovered fatally wounded early this morning in . . .

It could happen, I knew. Almost every evening deaths like that were part of the national news.

"And if these children learn to just say no . . ." I thought that voice belonged to the wife of our high school principal.

It was a great idea, but at the moment I couldn't name many kids in our senior class that I'd ever heard answer no to "Want to try some?" It was usually booze, but I had to admit it was drugs, too. I often wondered why Amy, Mary Agnes, and I hadn't tried anything more dangerous than rum and Coke, but maybe that wasn't so safe, either. "Just say no" made refusing sound so simple. There was no "just" if a bunch of kids were on a weekend bash. Someone should tell the Concerned Parents about the real world outside their backyards.

I wanted to stop the news reports flashing in my head, but the voices from the other room kept them going: "You know where it's the worst? Down at the Pits!"

"I can handle the pot and stuff, Trace, but I'm scared about the drinking. I can't seem to stop." Stanley was crouched at the edge of the Pits, where there was a straight drop down to the water.

"Just say no," I told him.

"Don't you understand?" He was almost crying. "Can't you help me?" Before I could answer he was gone, the sound of his body hitting the water almost muffled by the music from somebody's boom box.

What if he didn't come back up? The Pits were dangerous, even in daylight, with boulders hidden beneath the water. Only the craziest kids actually dived in. Where could I find help? I peered into the black water. Was it an accident? Or did Stanley do it on purpose?

I stopped folding fliers and walked over to the window.

"Of course," Mom was explaining at length to the women in the living room, "marching around town isn't going to get rid of the pushers that slip into our town, but at least it will make citizens aware. . . ."

I thought how Dad had kidded Mom, at first, about dirty old men lurking on street corners. If I'd been half a friend of Stanley's, I'd have shouted back to Mom, "Pushers don't have to slip into town. Pushers are around already, and they aren't dirty old men lurking on street corners, they're your own children!"

But, of course, I didn't. I just kept on imagining what could happen.

I was having trouble making out the printing on the name tags of my former classmates. After all, people change in ten years, and I hadn't been back for a class reunion before. I reached for my glasses and looked around.

"Is Mary Agnes here?"

"Mary Agnes?" Boyd asked. "Haven't you heard? Remember how inseparable she and Stanley Prentice were senior year? Well, she got involved with drugs and then she started writing bad checks. She's serving a sentence for that or prostitution or both. And Stanley . . ."

"How are you coming with those fliers, Tracy?" Mom was standing in the doorway. I hadn't heard the others leave.

"I'm almost finished," I said and walked back to the pile of unfolded papers. I began again, folding each sheet once over from the right and once over from the left, creasing the fold and adding it to the pile.

Mom sat down and watched me with that blank look she always wore when she wasn't thinking about what she was seeing. There was something in her face, something in the way she was lying back in the chair, something in the way she was smiling, sort of self-satisfied, that made me blurt out, "It's not going to do any good, you know. The marching and the placards and all this stuff I'm folding. I tried to tell you that before. There's nothing wrong with it, but the only people who'll pay any attention are adults and other parents."

She didn't get angry and she didn't tell me I was wrong; instead, she nodded slowly. "I think I know what you mean, Trace. I was listening to what we were saying in there. So many words. So many good intentions. All just talk, wasn't it?"

For once, it sounded as if Mom was actually asking my opinion, wanting to know what I thought, not just expecting me to agree or disagree.

I did something then that I hadn't done since junior high. I walked over and sat down on the floor next to her and for a minute I understood what Grandma Ida had said about a daughter feeling like a mother. Mom looked as if she needed comforting, but when she reached out and smoothed my hair back from my face, I knew it was I who needed help.

I didn't try to stop my words. "Have you ever had to make a choice that means no matter what you decide, you'll end up hurting someone?"

"Yes."

"So, how do you decide?"

"You make a leap of faith and keep your fingers crossed. You have to believe that what may be painful now will be best in the future." She smiled down at me. "Does that make any sense?"

I nodded. The repotting must have been as painful for her and Dad as it had been, at first, for me. And this *was* that future, and it *was* better.

"Tracy, what's wrong? I don't mean to pry, but is there anything I can do?"

"I'm not sure. It's like this. If I do one thing, I'm going to lose at least one friend, but if I don't do it, a friend may get hurt. And if I don't do anything, I'm going to feel terrible the rest of my life."

"Is it that serious? That important?"

"It's that important." I had tried to pretend it wasn't, but I'd only been lying to myself. I took a deep breath and before I could chicken out I said, "It's Stanley!"

Somehow, once I'd said his name, I felt as if I'd explained everything, but Mom looked at me, totally puzzled. I could see it was going to be even harder than I'd thought. I might even then have tried to wiggle out of what I'd begun, if those mental pictures of Stanley's possible nonfuture hadn't been so vivid.

"I think he's an alcoholic! I know he's a junkie. I'm afraid he's a pusher. . . ." I was almost crying, and I hated myself for it. "Somebody's got to stop him! Somebody has to help him!"

"Oh, Tracy." Mom slid out of the chair, knelt on the floor beside me and put her arms around me. "How terribly, terribly sad! How long have you known? Why didn't you tell me?" Her voice held no anger, but was so full of tenderness that I felt like a little girl again and buried my head in her shoulder until I was sure my voice was steady enough to try to answer her question.

"I don't know how long I've known, but you were always so busy—with your new book and the research on drugs and then the parade and the pamphlets and all. Mary Agnes and Amy and I tried to stop him, but he wouldn't listen to us, and he just kept on drowning himself in booze every chance he got. I wanted to tell you several times, but, Mom, I couldn't. Stanley trusted me!" I finally ran out of breath and words.

"Trusted you? Or needed you?"

"Is there a difference?"

"A big difference. Trust is sharing. Need is taking."

"But I believed him when he said not to worry about what he was doing. I didn't think he'd lie to me."

"I'm sure the real Stanley wouldn't. The drugs . . . the alcohol . . . that's where the lies come from. The only thing that can help Stanley is the truth. And that's what's so important about what you're doing now with me—sharing the truth."

Sharing sure sounded better than snitching.

"What made you finally decide to tell me, Tracy?"

That was the trouble with Mom. First she wanted to know why I *didn't* tell her and now she wanted to know why I *did* tell her. I thought about calling her on that, but I really didn't want to argue anymore.

"I'm telling you because I'm afraid of what might happen to Stanley when your CPAD finds out about him. And because I thought you'd know what to do." I stared at my sneakers. "And because I can trust you. . . ."

Why was it so difficult to tell her what I really felt?

"But mostly, I guess, because you're my mom."

I'm not sure how long we sat on the floor and talked, but I told her everything—how I'd tried to help Stanley, how I'd covered for him, fibbed for him, rescued him down in Maple Grove one night, loaned him money, and even that I was hiding his book of buyers for him up in my bedroom, though I didn't say how I'd gotten it. I even told her about the rum and Coke. I was sure any other mother would have screamed or fainted or gulped down a handful of aspirins, but Mom just looked at me and smiled like when an answer that you didn't know you knew suddenly pops into your head.

"What are we going to do?" I pushed my hair off my forehead. I'm sure I looked as wretched as I felt.

Mom stood up and pulled me up with her. "I'm only a mother, Tracy, but together we ought to be able to figure something out."

I had never realized before how comfortable the word "we" could sound, and then I realized that the "we" had been missing in Mom's and my vocabulary for all too long.

"Actually," she said, as we sat down at the kitchen table, the place where our long-ago serious talks had always taken place, "It's a matter of sorting our alternatives."

"We can't go to the police. They'd arrest Stanley!"

"Is there any chance we could convince Stanley that he ought to go to Mavis and Bob for help?" Mom answered her own question almost as quickly as she asked it. "But I don't suppose he thinks he needs help, does he?"

"It's certainly not up to us to go to his parents, is it?"

"Well, we really owe it to Stanley to tell him what we're going to do. He may want to tell his parents himself. Maybe that's why he gave you that book. He was asking for help."

I didn't dare tell Mom that Stanley was running from a cop and didn't want to get caught with the list of all the kids he'd been selling to and buying from.

Instead, I said, "I think he was good and scared when

he gave me The Book, but you know Stanley, Mom. It's a game with him—to outsmart his folks, teachers, cops, everybody. And he can."

"Even you?"

"He cons me. But I know I'm being conned, and he knows I know I'm being conned. That's the way Stanley is."

I'm not sure Mom understood what I was trying to say. I'm not sure I did myself. Mom kept watching me as I talked, as if waiting for *me* to come up with a solution for Stanley.

"I don't think the answer is for me to go talk to Mavis about him, do you?"

She was asking me! I think my eyes must have grown two sizes larger.

"It'd probably make her feel awfully bad, don't you think?"

We were asking each other questions! We weren't arguing. We weren't getting mad at each other. I couldn't believe it.

"Do you want to know what I think?" The idea had just occurred to me, and I was sure if I didn't say it right then I'd never have the courage to say it again.

"Yes."

"I think *I'm* the one who has to do something, not you." Mom hadn't looked at me that way since I came home with an A in eighth grade math. I went on before I could lose what courage I had left. "I'll go talk to Stanley. Then I'll go with him to talk to his mother."

"What if he won't go with you?"

"He'll go! I have The Book."

16

I DIDN'T HAVE TO FIND STANLEY. HE CAME TO me with the list of marchers Mom said he'd have. He pulled up to the curb just as I was coming out of the house.

"Hey, Trace. I need my Book back and I want to ask you something."

I knew what was coming. I knew the very words. I could have said them before he did.

"Would you do me a favor?" Stanley's bounce-back powers were amazing. Once again, he looked nothing like the kid I'd seen the night before, and even more astounding, he seemed to assume that I'd forgotten all about his terror.

"What this time?" Why did I bother to ask? This was a broken record, the same old runaround.

"Well, last night, after you dropped me off, on the way home I got picked up for possession." He didn't sound embarrassed; he sounded as if it were a joke.

"Possession of what?" I almost hoped it was pot. The threat of jail might knock some sense into him.

"Beer. No big deal, but Dad will probably turn it into

a major production. If I pay my own fine . . . So could you, maybe, lend me . . ."

"*No!*" I shouted. "No more!" I added just in case he hadn't heard my first refusal. "I'm not your enabler."

He started to laugh. "Enabler?" he repeated. "You've been reading that stuff you've been folding, haven't you? But come on. Get real. Be a sport. I just need a twenty and I'll pay you back next week, honest."

If he hadn't laughed, I might have kept my mouth shut. Instead, I stared just over his left shoulder, took a deep breath and said, very slowly, "It's all over, Stanley. We're going to go talk to your folks . . . about everything. Blackouts, pot, using, selling—the whole bit." I knew I was sounding like something out of a bad TV show, but I couldn't think of any other way to say what I meant.

For a minute he looked at me as if I were speaking some kind of language that was completely foreign to him. Then he turned on a weak glimmer of his normal Stanley-charm. "Okay, okay. Give The Book back and we'll forget the money." He had stopped laughing.

"You can forget The Book until after you tell your mom and dad that you've been totally out to lunch since sometime last spring, or longer than that, for all I know." I opened the car door and sat down beside him.

"You have to be crazy. They're my *parents*—remember? It'd kill them if they thought I was in any real trouble. And I'm not. Honest. Trace, last night really did scare me. I've decided to stop doing pot. It's not like I *have* to smoke it or anything." If he hadn't sounded so sincere, I might have believed him.

"It's *because* they're your parents that you have to tell them. And what about the next party when somebody offers *you* a joint . . . or a drink? Come on, Stanley, maybe you can con yourself, but this is me. What are you waiting for? Let's get it over with." I knew that if we sat talking long enough all my determination would disappear as fast as his promises.

"If you think I'm going to tell anybody anything . . ."

"You have one big choice, buddy-boy. You tell them or I give them The Book—if I don't give it to the police first."

That's when he looked at me as if he hated me, and for the only time in my life, I was almost scared of him. "Yeah? And how are you going to like it when I tell your mom about those little rum and Coke sessions with Amy and Mary Agnes?"

I laughed; I couldn't help it. Stanley sounded just like the little kid he used to be—"If you tell on me, I'll tell on you." "For somebody so smart, you can be incredibly stupid. Mom knows all about that and she knows all about you. You're a prime example of why the 'cultural evenings' won't happen again. Now, let's move it."

He didn't look at me. Maybe it was because I laughed at him instead of launching into another lecture that was beginning to sound phony even to me.

"What made you narc on me?" I couldn't tell whether he was so angry he couldn't get the words out of his mouth or if he was scared.

"Because you won't do anything for yourself!" I almost shouted.

I was wrong! I was all wrong! I knew it the minute I heard myself saying the words. "I didn't mean that, Stanley." I grabbed his arm. "It isn't that you *won't.* It's that you *can't!* Don't you see? That's why I'm going with you. Because . . ." I tried to think of the right words, "because there's only one Stanley, and I don't want to waste him."

He didn't answer, and we sat there without saying another word until the silence grew so long my ears started ringing. Finally, staring straight ahead, he started the car, and we drove slowly over to his house.

I knew, though, if it hadn't been for my having Stanley's book, I might never have forced him into talking to his mother. As it was, I ended up doing most of the telling, but he didn't try very hard to deny anything.

When I left, his mother was on the phone with his dad and Stanley was slumped in a chair staring at the floor. He didn't look up or even say good-bye.

On the walk home, I tried to forget the look on his mother's face and instead tried to remember the hope in her voice when she said, "You know, Stanley, we love you no matter what. And we'll find help. I promise. Help for us all."

She didn't cry. I wanted to.

Telling Mom hadn't been easy, nor had telling Stanley's mom, but I knew I had to face Mary Agnes and Amy and that wasn't going to be any easier. After I checked in with Mom and told her what had happened, I called Mary Agnes and told her to meet me at Amy's. You never know how friends are going to act when they're in complete shock. Mary Agnes hugged me, something she'd never done before.

"I wanted to tell somebody, too," she admitted, "but I don't know . . . I guess . . . I was afraid to get mixed up in it."

Amy looked as if I'd hit her over the head with a Coke bottle. "Maybe CPADs and marches aren't so stupid after all. But what's going to happen to Stanley?"

"I'm not sure," I said. "But I don't think he'll ever speak to me again."

From the looks on their faces, I knew they agreed with me.

What did happen to Stanley was that when school started he was in Saint Louis in some kind of rehabilitation center. He hadn't called before he left, and I was kind of glad because I wouldn't have known what to say.

Mom explained everything to Dad, of course, and they both tried their best to make me feel comfortable about what I'd done. When the CPAD marched, they even walked beside Stanley's mom and dad.

I finally started feeling better when a postcard with a picture of the Saint Louis Arch came sometime in October. The note on the back said, "See you at Thanksgiving, Turkey." Maybe Stanley didn't totally hate me after all.

One Saturday, not long after that, Mom emerged from her study with a box full of file folders.

"Tracy, would you please take this down to the basement? Put it on the top shelf in the storage room while I pack up the rest."

"Sure," I said. "What is it?"

She hadn't said much about how her book was going, and I thought I should show a little interest in what she was doing. Besides, she'd changed. In just a couple of months, she'd stopped being a prodding, pushy pain in the neck and had become a kind of neat human being. Our Saturdays together, while Dad was out prowling the prairie, had even become rather special.

"It's the drug research. I've given up trying to write about it and I'm not sure it ever belonged on the Help Yourself list." She set the box on the table. "Stanley could never have helped himself. He needed someone like you."

"You're not quitting, are you? The series, I mean." I couldn't imagine my mother not writing.

"No, of course not." She walked over and gave me a one-arm hug. "I'm going back to daughters. And do you know what the first word of the book will be?"

"I have no idea," I said, hoping I sounded as curious as I felt.

"HELP!" she shouted, and disappeared into her study.

I laughed and picked up the box.